DRUID BLOOD

DRUID BLOOD

A JUNKYARD DRUID PREQUEL NOVEL

M.D. MASSEY

Modern Digital Publishing

Austin, Texas

Modern Digital Publishing
P.O. Box 682
Dripping Springs, Texas 78620

Druid Blood/ M.D. Massey. — 2nd ed.

Contents

Preface

The book you hold in your hands (or digital hands, as it may be) is a sort of prequel to my new adult urban fantasy novel, *Junkyard Druid*. It features the same protagonist, one Colin McCool, a druid-trained warrior and champion of the human race. It also features other characters from the *Junkyard Druid* series, including Finn, Maureen, and Colin's then very much alive girlfriend, Jesse.

Alas, it is also the very first novel I ever finished, and one I originally wrote for a young adult audience. I was learning as I wrote this novel, and upon editing it for this second edition, I can honestly say that it's not my *best* work. However, I also have to say that it's a favorite of mine among the novels I've written thus far.

Sure, it's a little rough; it has some issues with tense and point of view, and there are a few minor plot continuity errors that I just couldn't bring myself to fix (because I'm sentimental like that). But it's a fun story to read, and if you're like me and you enjoy reading both YA and adult fantasy fiction, I think you'll enjoy it as much as I enjoyed writing it.

But, more importantly, this story informs the reader regarding important events in the saga of Colin McCool. It serves as a sort of origin story for him, one that I hope readers who are new to the character will appreciate. And it provides a glimpse into Colin and Jesse's relationship, long before they suffer tragedy and heartbreak in the worst way imaginable.

Which brings up an interesting point: one of the reasons why I decided to re-release this novel. This story marks what is mostly a happy and carefree time in young Colin's life. This is the point where he and Jesse move into that period he describes as "living in a J.K. Rowling novel." And, because Colin's story becomes so tragic later on, I just couldn't bury this singular, mostly happy chapter in his life among the detritus of my own personal slush pile.

So, I sincerely hope you enjoy this book. And if you're one of those readers who simply can't stand YA novels, then by all means feel free to skip this installment in the Colin McCool series. It won't hurt my feelings one bit if you do—but if that's your choice, then I do suggest you skip forward to *Junkyard Druid* for a more adult-oriented treatment of these characters. Which brings me to my final purpose for writing this preface...

Parents, listen up. I know a lot of younger children read YA novels, and I know plenty of pre-teens bought this book when I first released it to the YA market. However, you should know that if your child previously read this book and you're expecting them to continue the same profanity-free, "absent of sexual situations" story in the *Junkyard Druid* series, you will be sadly disappointed. There's a reason why I chose to relaunch this character in a new adult novel series, and that's because I wanted the leeway and freedom to explore more mature topics and stories with Colin McCool. So, please think twice before you let your younger kids read the Junkyard Druid novels.

M.D. Massey

P.S. I have more *free* stuff for you on my website at MDMassey.com. Head on over and subscribe to my newsletter for another free book and additional, exclusive content!

Prologue

Note to readers:

I've hounded Colin time and again about telling this part of his and Jesse's story, but he's been rather pig-headed regarding the whole thing. It's understandable, considering what he's been through. Yet, I know that someday he'll go down in history as a pivotal figure in the Great War to come, and because of that people will want to know how he went from a chubby, snot-nosed kid to the druid-trained warrior he is today.

For lack of Colin's willingness to tell his own story, it falls to me to write this tale down for the sake of posterity. I suppose it's also therapeutic for me to record these events, because doing so will allow me to reflect on somewhat happier times, when Jesse was still around. I do miss that girl. She wasn't the first, nor the last, pupil I've lost to the Eternal War, but she does hold a spot among the nearest and dearest to me... of that, there is no doubt.

That being said, it's a sad state of affairs when the tale of a boy being hunted by a two thousand-year-old vampire qualifies as a memory of "happier times." I just hope I'll be able to prepare him for what's to come, because that poor lad has yet to experience his last heartbreak.

-Finnegas the Seer

Colin ran through a dark forest. The last rays of daylight peeked through the thick overhead canopy in weak sunbeams that did little to light his way. He heard his pursuers behind him. Their footsteps were a quiet, but insistent, padding—just at the edge of his hearing, barely enough to let him know they were there. But they *were* there, and Colin had the sense that they were *hungry*. He dug deep and put on more speed, but his lungs burned, his legs were on fire, and he knew he couldn't keep this pace much longer.

And he was terrified. Every direction he looked, he saw eyes peering at him out of the darkness. Round red eyes, slitted yellow eyes, eyes that shone like a fire in the dark, grey-green eyes that glowed with an eerie luminescence, and sick bloodshot eyes that he shouldn't have even been able to see in the darkness. There were hundreds of them, leering hungrily, as he ran.

He kept running.

And as he looked back over his shoulder to gauge whatever meager lead he might have had on his pursuers, Colin tripped and fell over a tree root that he swore hadn't been there a second ago. Although he wanted to give up, he knew that if he stopped running he was a goner. *Keep going,* he thought. *I just gotta make it home.* Spitting out rotten leaves and other forest debris, he jumped to his feet and kept going.

Looking over his shoulder he saw them, briefly, in the shadows. The things that chased him bounded after him in great huge leaps, and the forerunners were two dark feline shapes that moved like liquid night. He also saw three imp-like creatures with sharp teeth and claws, each wearing caps that dripped with blood, splashing on the leaves and forest floor as they ran. The imps cackled at Colin and called to each other like hyenas on the hunt as they closed in on him.

Another creature pursued in the shadows behind them. Although it was the smallest, that one was the most menacing by far. There was a palpable evil coming off the thing in waves, and Colin felt sick to his stomach each time he felt its presence.

The creature was man-like in form, but the shadows and darkness obscured its features, making it all the more terrible to behold. Most frightening of all was the way it moved—just like something Colin had seen in a late night horror film. It would be still for a moment, then the form would flicker and cover ten feet or more in a blink. That scared the boy more than anything he'd seen, so he turned his eyes back to the path ahead and ran for all he was worth.

A light appeared through the trees ahead, and Colin thanked his lucky stars as he made a beeline for it. However, it quickly vanished from sight and he found himself running blindly in the dark once more. As he leapt over yet another tree limb that seemed to claw at his feet and ankles, he glimpsed the light again. Believing that safety was near, he bounded ahead, heart pounding, in a burst of energy that gave him a slight but welcome lead on his pursuers.

Without warning, the ground gave way beneath Colin's feet and he fell into a cave-like opening in the ground. He landed hard after falling a good ten feet to the cavern floor, twisting his ankle badly underneath him. Despite the pain he quickly oriented himself, finding little around him but darkness. For all he knew, it might have ended a few feet away, or it could have gone to infinity.

Writhing in pain on the ground, holding his injured leg, he gazed at the dim circle of light overhead that represented his only escape. As he looked around frantically, attempting to get his bearings, Colin noticed small points of light flashing into existence in the darkness around him, like fireflies at dusk. But as they materialized, it became apparent that the lights weren't fireflies, but *eyes*. Hundreds of them, blinking and staring out at him from the darkness of the cavern.

Colin looked up again at the opening above, seeking some means of escape, but his way was now blocked by dark shapes who crouched menacingly around the space. Then Colin heard a grating metallic sound, and realized his pursuers were closing the opening and trapping him inside. His only source of light faded as the cavern mouth closed like a huge eye, blinking shut. As the circle of light he stood in drew closer and closer, the eyes that stared all around him began to close in with the encroaching darkness.

Finally, only a sliver of light remained... and then it was gone. As hundreds of pairs of glowing eyes converged on him, Colin screamed with terror into the blackness.

1

The alarm clock went off with a high-pitched scream that matched Colin's own. He awoke with a start, heart beating out of his chest and his sheets soaked in sweat. Looking around and sighing with relief upon realizing he was in his bedroom at home, Colin flopped his head back down on his pillow, taking deep breaths in an effort to slow his rapidly beating heart. Strangely, he couldn't recall the dream that had frightened him so badly during his sleep.

Just another nightmare. He shut off the alarm, noticing the time.

9:28 am. That meant the alarm had been going off for almost 30 minutes. Thankfully it was Saturday, which meant he could stay in bed a few more minutes. He rested his head on the pillow again, then groaned and sat up with a start.

Oh crud, the game! Colin jumped out of bed and snatched up some pants and a baseball jersey from a pile beside his bed. *Odd that mom hasn't been on me to put away my stuff,* he reflected as he got dressed.

That stray thought caused him to pause, despite the fact that he was already late. Something nagged at him that was just on the edge of his awareness, like an itch he couldn't scratch. *No sense worrying about it now,* he thought. *I'm sure it'll come to me on the way to the game.* Shaking off his confusion, he threw on some socks and sneakers, grabbed his cleats and his favorite bat, and flew down the staircase to make a beeline for the front door.

Just as his fingers hit the doorknob, he heard a stern yet loving voice call from the kitchen. "Wait just a minute, mister. You are *not* leaving this house without a decent breakfast."

Colin turned to see his mother looking sternly at him from the kitchen entrance. She'd already made breakfast for him, set out on the breakfast table like a picture from *Martha Stewart Living*. There were stacks of perfect, fluffy pancakes drizzled in melted butter and syrup, bacon fried to crisp perfection, and scrambled eggs that he knew were expertly cooked to a light and delicate consistency. The smell was overpowering, and made his stomach growl.

Seeing the meal his mom had prepared for him, he felt a pang of guilt for trying to leave before checking in with her. It had been just the two of them for a while now, but Colin still felt guilty about leaving his mom alone on Saturday mornings, since Saturday breakfast had always been a family affair when his dad had still been around. Besides that, Colin's mom had always been the doting sort, and since his dad had died Colin knew she channeled her grief into caring for him.

Despite the fact that he also missed his dad terribly, lately Colin had found that he preferred distraction over feeling the loss. Beyond any doubt, he and his dad had been very close, but recently he'd been thinking less and less about his father. He kept meaning to pull out their photo album to reminisce, but whenever he started to look for the album he found some excuse to put it off another day. Colin felt guilty about it, and wondered if he was forgetting about his father entirely. He made a mental note to look for the album when he got back from the game, and turned his attention to more immediate matters.

"Sorry, Mom, but I'm late and I have to leave right now or I'll miss the first inning. The team is really counting on me to show up."

It sounded strange coming out of his mouth, but in fact his team *was* counting on him. Colin had become the star of his baseball team this season, with an impressive fifteen home runs thus far. In fact, no one was more surprised by his performance than Colin himself. Although he'd experienced quite a growth spurt over the last year, he'd always been a pudgy kid—not very coordinated, picked last on teams. So even he was surprised at his recent home run streak.

What made it even stranger was the fact that his best friend Jesse had become another team standout of late, taking over as starting pitcher and nudging Bryce Johnson to the team's relief position. Neither of them had ever been exceptionally gifted at sports, which was one of the reasons they'd become friends; all those years of bench-sitting had provided them with plenty of time to bond. He supposed it was possible they'd both simply begun to realize their latent athletic talent at the same time. Shaking off yet another worrisome thought, he took the pancake, bacon, and egg sandwich that his mom shoved into his hands, scarfing down half of it in a single bite.

His mom tsked at him and sighed. "Well, I suppose a sandwich will have to do. Hit a home run for me today, okay, champ?" She leaned in and kissed him on the cheek, something that Colin tolerated only when his friends weren't around.

"Thanks, Mom—I'll be home right after the game, unless Jesse's parents take us out for burgers and shakes." He zipped out of the house, grabbing the keys to his new 650 supersport motorcycle just before slamming the door behind him.

As he donned his helmet and hopped on his bike, the fact that his mom was letting him drive a motorcycle nagged at him. It *did* seem kind of dangerous that he should have a "four-stroke, 636 cc, two-wheeled instrument of awesomeness" (as the guy at the dealership called it) as his first vehicle, but that's what made it so awesome. The really cool thing was that he didn't need his mom to drive him around town and to his games anymore.

Anyway, these days she was *way* too busy with her art gallery openings to come see him play. It made Colin happy to see her pursuing her dream of being an artist, since she'd had to quit art school and take a job as a legal secretary when his dad had died. Now that her art career was taking off, soon she'd be able to stay home, paint, and follow her dream. All Colin cared about was that it made her happy; she'd been depressed for a very long time after his dad had died.

Once again, Colin tried to remember what his dad had looked like, but he couldn't summon a clear memory. Strapping his lucky bat to the bike's handlebars with a bungee cord, he shrugged it off and revved up the engine, peeling out of his driveway and popping a wheelie on his way down the street.

Eager to get to the ball field, Colin zoomed down Main Street at speeds that were most definitely illegal. Zipping in and out of traffic and around cars that were in his way, he ran a red light at 4th and Main. Narrowly avoiding a car coming from the other direction, he gunned it and sped off through the intersection.

Within moments of running the red light Colin heard sirens

behind him, and a quick glance in his mirrors showed a police cruiser on his tail. He pulled over to the curb a half a block later, glancing at his watch for the time. *Just ten minutes till the game starts*, he thought. *Plenty of time.*

The officer walked up, his hand resting on his sidearm. At first he looked really serious, but then a big smile crept across his face. "Late for the big game today, Colin?"

"Good morning, Officer Haney—sorry about that red light. Yes, sir, I am. The team is really counting on me today and I don't want to miss the first inning."

"Well, we can't let our star player be late for the big game. Aren't you supposed to set the home run record again today?"

"If I get a home run, yes sir. It'll be the third time this season." Again, Colin marveled at just how ludicrous it was for him to be the star player on the team. Just last year he'd gotten made fun of for sucking his thumb, and kids in gym class had called him "Colin McBoobs." Funny how quickly things had turned around for him.

Office Haney smiled. "Alright, a police escort it is, then. Follow me, and we'll get you to the field on time."

"Thanks, Officer Haney."

As the police car took off with lights and sirens blaring, Colin started his bike and peeled out after him. He gunned it and swerved into the right lane, cutting off an old lady in a Lexus—a move that earned him a rude gesture and a horn blast from the old lady. He looked back over his shoulder and waved at her. "Sorry!" he exclaimed, then turned back to follow the police car rapidly leaving him behind.

As he turned back around, he saw that a homeless man had appeared out of nowhere directly in front of him. *Where'd he come from?* Colin thought. *I could swear he wasn't there a second ago.*

Time seemed to slow as Colin and his bike bore down on the old man, and he yanked the handle bars while leaning hard to avoid hitting him. As if he were watching a movie in slow motion, he saw every detail of the scene flash before him as he swerved to avoid hitting the old man.

"Hang on to that bat, kid!" the old homeless guy yelled, as Colin flew past him. Strangely, the man didn't even flinch as Colin narrowly missed hitting him, despite the fact that 600 pounds of motorcycle and rider almost mowed him down.

Guy must be on drugs, Colin thought. *Why didn't he jump out of the way?*

Time sped up once again as he swerved off the road and up onto the sidewalk, where his front wheel lodged into Mrs. O'Malley's white picket fence.

As the wheel hit the fence, the bike stopped moving but Colin didn't. The momentum catapulted him into the air, over the fence, through Mrs. O'Malley's bushes on the other side of the fence, and straight at the strangest-looking little person Colin had ever seen.

2

Time slowed again as Colin flew through the air toward the small, strange-looking man. *Wow*, he thought, taking in his surroundings while airborne at 30 miles an hour, *I feel like I'm in The Matrix.* Knowing he had to land sometime, and that landing wouldn't be all that pleasant, Colin decided to enjoy the moment by taking in the details of his unintended target.

The little man Colin was about to flatten wore a rather smart green waistcoat over a crisp white dress shirt, along with a black derby, brown tweed trousers, black calfskin gloves, and a pair of highly-polished black dress shoes. And while he obviously took great care with the quality of his wardrobe, to Colin the man looked *very* strange.

As Colin calmly noted the small man's clothes, something else stood out to him that was very peculiar. Even stranger than what the man wore was what he had in his hands. It was a large grey rock with unfamiliar symbols chiseled into it, and those symbols glowed faintly as the little man turned it over and over in his hands.

The last thing Colin thought while he flew through the air at breakneck speed was to wish that he'd eaten a proper breakfast, because this was turning out to be a really crappy day and a good breakfast always cheered him up. Upon the completion of that thought, Colin's flight abruptly ended when his helmeted head smashed into the rock in the strange little man's hands.

Colin opened his eyes and found himself staring at the gray sky through a canopy of brown and yellow leaves, when just moments before they'd been lush and green. His head hurt like the dickens, but taking a personal inventory, he appeared to be all in one piece. He removed his now cracked and ruined helmet, thankful that the worst injury he'd received from the collision was a relatively minor headache.

Colin sat up as the little man dusted himself off several feet away. "Well, you've gone and mucked that up—yes you have, old Brogan.

Oh, yes indeed," the little man muttered to himself, brushing leaves and twigs from his pants and waistcoat.

"Hey, mister, are you alright?" Colin asked, with genuine concern in his voice.

The little man turned toward Colin and jumped, and his eyes grew big as saucers. He made fists of his little hands and rubbed his eyes, then placed his fists on his hips and frowned.

"Oh, now, isn't this just a lovely little mess old Brogan's gotten into. You can see me, lad, and without an adder stone to boot? Oh, I'm ruined for sure! Now, where did me Blarney stone go?" He patted his pockets as if the large stone could have fallen into one during the crash.

Colin rubbed his head and winced. "Look, I don't know anything about any stones, except for the one you were carrying. Here, let me help you find it."

Colin crawled around on his hands and knees, searching the hedges for the rock. He finally located it a few feet away. As he grasped the stone, the symbols flared brightly and he felt a small shock where his hands made contact. Momentarily, his vision sharpened and his head cleared; the effect was a lot like downing five cups of espresso. Colin knew this, because he and Jesse had done that recently, after her dad bought a new espresso machine.

Wondering if he'd damaged the rock in the crash, Colin handled it with care as he passed it back to man who called himself Brogan. "Here you go, mister—but be careful, because that thing just shocked me."

The little man took the stone from Colin, and a grim look crossed his strange little face. "Oh, you're quite the helper, aren't you now? Thanks, me boy."

He stared at Colin for a moment, tapping his foot and looking at him as if he was deciding something of no small import. Then, he muttered something unintelligible and continued speaking as if he'd never paused.

"Well, then, I'll just be getting back to what I was doing, before you so rudely interrupted me." With a tip of his hat, he hurried off through a gap in the bushes, muttering to himself about calamities and catastrophes all the way.

Colin followed him out of the hedgerow by crawling as near to the ground as he could to avoid getting scratched. When he exited the hedge, it was as if his whole world had changed from one moment to the next.

For starters, his motorcycle was nowhere to be found. Instead of his bike, there sat a crummy old 50 cc scooter with chipped paint, bald tires, and a severely bent front rim. Colin was furious that someone had taken his motorcycle and left him with this piece of junk, but he decided that he didn't have time to worry about it. He'd just find Officer Haney later and file a report on the stolen motorbike.

He still needed a ride to the game, so he reached for his new phone to call his mom. But in the place of his brand new smart phone he instead found a regular old crummy flip phone, which incidentally looked as though it had taken some damage in the crash. *Okay, this is getting weird*, he thought.

Thankfully, whoever had stolen his motorcycle had left his bat behind. Colin walked over to retrieve it and noticed they'd left his bungee cord, too, and had used it to tie the bat to the scooter. *This is really freaking me out*, he thought to himself. *What the heck is going on here?*

After retrieving his bat, he stood and finally got a good look at his surroundings; downtown Farmersville appeared to have undergone a radical transformation. Where before there had been neatly trimmed bushes and hedges, sparkling glass storefronts, spotless sidewalks and streets, manicured lawns, and brightly painted homes, now there was a town that looked like a war zone. Broken-down cars were parked at random next to and at times over the curbs, trash was strewn everywhere, windows were smashed in homes and storefronts, grass, trees, and bushes were brown and unkempt, weeds poked up through cracks in the sidewalks, and the overall appearance was of a town that had been long neglected and disused.

Much as the little man had done just a few minutes before, Colin rubbed his eyes with his fists. When he opened them again, the mess remained. *What the heck happened to my town?* he thought. Confused and a little frightened, he plopped down in the dry brown grass while his mind frantically sought a reasonable explanation for the sudden change in his surroundings.

As he contemplated recent events, Colin began chewing his thumbnail in earnest. He knew it was a childish habit, but it always seemed to help him think more clearly. As a kid he'd been teased relentlessly about it, so these days he'd replaced the habit with chewing his thumbnail since it drew less negative attention. He still got called "thumbsucker" on occasion, though.

"Maybe I was out for a lot longer than I thought," he mumbled around his thumb. No, that didn't make sense; at least, not any more sense than what his eyes were already telling him. Could he have injured his head in the crash? Colin thought it was possible, but he'd never heard of a concussion having such side effects. When kids got hit in the head in baseball, usually they just complained of blurry vision and headaches.

No, there had to be another explanation for it... and he had a sneaking suspicion the strange little man with the rock would know what was going on. Looking around to see where he had gone, he noticed his friends and neighbors going about their business in an almost zombie-like fashion.

There was Mr. Morris who ran the pharmacy, sweeping his front walk with a broomstick that had no bristles. Across the street, he could see Dean the barber through the window of his shop, going through the motions of cutting imaginary hair on Mr. O'Malley's bald head, and with no scissors or clippers in his hands besides. And there went Jesse's dad, driving an old beat up station wagon that appeared to be on its last leg. But hadn't she said they'd just gotten a new car? It was all very confusing, and Colin somehow knew he'd never get any answers unless he found that leprechaun...

Leprechaun? Now where had that idea come from? Everyone knew there were no such things as leprechauns; but with the way this day was turning out, it wouldn't surprise him to find out they were real after all. He scanned his surroundings, turning in a slow circle until he saw a flash of green heading down the alley behind the barber shop.

Colin's hands clutched his lucky bat tightly as he sped off after the bizarre little man. He was determined to catch up with him, and when he did, he would have some answers.

3

Skidding around the corner as his sneakers lost traction in a puddle of motor oil, Colin used the bat like a ski pole to stay on his feet. He caught a glimpse of the little man rounding the corner ahead, and as he righted himself he put on speed to catch up. At first it seemed there'd be little challenge in catching Brogan, considering how much longer Colin's legs were; however, the speed of his prey surprised and baffled him. It seemed that at every turn that Brogan was always just ahead of him, but far enough away that Colin never seemed to get any closer to catching him.

As Colin turned the next corner, he saw a small gloved hand disappearing under a manhole cover a few yards ahead. Skidding to a stop at the manhole, he was relieved to see that it had been left ajar—whether by mistake, or because Brogan expected to be coming back that way shortly, he wasn't sure. But it looked suspiciously like a trap to Colin, and he decided that rather than chasing the man down into the sewers, he'd hide until he came out again. He ducked behind some boxes and settled in to wait.

Within minutes, his patience was rewarded by the grinding of metal on metal. Ever so carefully, Colin peered over the box he hid behind and saw the little man crawling out of the manhole. Without a second thought, Colin jumped over the box to pounce on the leprechaun, pinning Brogan underneath him and placing the bat across his throat.

He immediately began peppering the elf-like man with questions. "What's going on? What did you do to me? What did you do to my town? How did all this happen? *Answer me!*"

Colin was actually quite surprised at his own ferocity, since he'd never acted like this before; well, not since he'd stood up to Corky Simpson in the fifth grade. But Colin was desperate for answers, because everything he'd seen since his accident had shaken him to his core. He told himself that anyone would have reacted similarly were they in his shoes. But he didn't really believe that, and wondered if he was changing right along with the town... and perhaps not for the better.

The leprechaun winced where the bat touched the bare skin of his neck. He and forced it away from his throat with a surprising amount of strength for someone so small.

"Okay now, laddie, okay. You've caught me fair and square, so you're entitled to your reward. Now, let me up and we can see to it straightaway." But with one look at the expression on the little man's face, Colin realized if he let him go now, he'd lose this chance forever.

"Uh-uh. First you talk, then I'll think about letting you go."

The little man's face fell in a feigned look of defeat. Then he flashed a warm smile and shrugged. "Well, you're a shrewd one, I'll give you that. And fierce as well—perhaps you've a bit of the blood of old King Fergus himself in you. Nonetheless, I couldn't give you any gold if I tried in me current state. But answers you shall have, so ask them."

Colin considered the words, and found the implications to be shocking. "So, you really are a leprechaun?"

The leprechaun nodded. "Yes. Brogan's the name, cobbling shoes and hiding gold is my game. I prefer to avoid granting wishes, if I can help it."

"But shouldn't you be wearing a long coat, with a four-leaf clover on it or something? And your accent isn't as thick as I'd have imagined, either."

Brogan grimaced. "Well now, if we're going to be flirting with stereotypes, I'll happily point out that you're a little tubby to be a ball player. Don't you think?"

"Very funny," Colin replied with a frown. "It so happens that I'm the star player on my team. So, I'm in good enough shape."

"Oh, are you now? And just when did this hidden athletic ability surface?" the strange little man asked with a smirk.

Colin paused, and thought back to when he'd first noticed his latent athletic skill. "About a month ago, I guess."

"And would that be about the time you got the motorbike? And when your mom's first art show opened? And when your buddy Jesse's family got the new house and car, right after her dad got his old job back, and with a promotion as well?"

Colin cocked his head and squinted with suspicion. "Yeah—so what?"

Brogan pushed back on the bat slightly, and Colin realized he'd been leaning on it a little too hard. He eased up a bit to allow the little man space to speak.

Brogan continued. "Doesn't it strike you as strange that everyone's fondest wish seemed to come true, and all around the same time? It's almost as if a *spell* came over your town, wouldn't you say?" He wriggled his fingers and waggled his eyebrows as he said the last bit, which would have been funny if Colin was in the mood to laugh.

Colin blinked his eyes as he thought about the last few weeks. "Well, I guess I never thought much about it until today."

"Until you bashed your head on me Blarney stone, you mean."

Colin rolled off of the wee man who called himself Brogan and slumped against a pile of boxes. "To be honest, before that happened I just never cared. But when I crawled out of the bushes, everything had changed."

Brogan sat up with a knowing smirk. "Indeed, because before that moment you were under the same spell as everyone else in this town. But once you laid hands on the Blarney stone, the spell was broken—at least for you, in any case."

"But isn't the Blarney stone in a castle in Ireland?"

Brogan looked at him appraisingly. "Well, you aren't as daft as you look. No, not that Blarney stone; I was speaking of me own *personal* Blarney stone. There's more than one, you know."

"No, I didn't." Brogan looked momentarily disappointed as Colin continued. "So, what gives with the spell and the Blarney stone? Did you cast the spell over the town?"

Brogan looked down at his hands, and actually seemed ashamed. "Aye, lad, indeed I did. But for the telling of that sad tale, I'll require a cup of tea to share it. Come on then, let's retire to me humble home and I'll tell you all about it."

Colin sat up and helped the leprechaun to his feet. The little man patted him on the arm. "You're a decent lad, for sure, and deserve an explanation. And, if me hunch serves correct, I believe we'll be able to help each other—once you know the whole story." He flipped the heavy manhole cover aside as if it was made from cardboard. Colin gasped.

Brogan winked at Colin over his shoulder. "Magic," the leprechaun stated simply. Then he dropped down the hole and disappeared.

Colin thought the leprechaun had escaped, but once he climbed down the manhole he realized that the little man hadn't given him the slip after all. Down below, Brogan stood in the light of an open doorway through the sewer wall. "Come now, lad, let's have some proper tea and discuss entering a mutually beneficial arrangement." He beckoned Colin through the door, and followed him inside.

After Colin and Brogan entered through the door, it shut behind them with a small *click*, leaving a flawlessly smooth wall behind. When Colin looked again it was as if there'd never been a door there at all. Glancing around the room, Colin was amazed by what he saw; it was as if someone had taken a modern condo and relocated it underground. He was obviously standing inside Brogan's home, but instead of looking like the hobbit-hole Colin might have expected, it had a definite bachelor pad feel to it. The living room looked as if it had been professionally decorated, and the fireplace was one of those fancy gas ones made of stainless steel and polished glass. The furniture was contemporary and colorful, and the decorations were more modern art than old country. Colin was impressed.

Brogan beamed with obvious pride, happy to be sharing his dwelling with a guest. "It's amazing what you can do with a credit card and an IKEA catalog." He gestured broadly, taking in the whole living area with a sweep of his hand. "Open concept. I stole the idea off of one of those home decorator shows." Brogan admired his home briefly then nodded once. "Wish I could give you the grand tour, but time is short. Come, let's have that tea now."

Colin followed Brogan into a modern kitchen, complete with stainless steel appliances and a huge kitchen island in the center. The leprechaun put a kettle on the stove and began preparing tea for them while he spoke.

"This story starts several years ago, with me minding me own business in retirement, living quietly underground. Some time ago, I'd decided to retire and move to the States. I wanted to enjoy small town life here in the southwest, and your town was just what I'd been looking for. So, there I was in the midst of enjoying me retirement, and that's when it all started. That's when *he* showed up." He paused as he brought out a beautiful silver tea service set. Once he'd prepared the china and kettle, he motioned for Colin to sit down at the nearby kitchen table, where he placed the tea along with a plate of Oreos and Girl Scout cookies.

The little man pointed at the plate. "Elves can't make them this good, not by a long shot. Help yourself, and by my beard and barrow, this is a gift freely given, with no ill meant toward you or yours in the gift, nor debt accrued in the acceptance." Colin looked at him strangely. "Means you can eat it without worrying about being spelled by me. You can never trust the fae, boy. Always remember that."

Colin nodded and began to say "thank you" when Brogan clapped a hand over his mouth.

"And never, ever, ever thank one of us. *Ever.* To you, what seems to be a simple thanks may be construed as incurring a debt to the fair folk—and that's something you never want to owe any of the *aes sídhe.*"

Colin looked perplexed. "Did you say 'a he-she'?"

Brogan scowled. "Not a 'he-she,' although the pronunciation's close enough. It's an old name for the fair folk, known as faeries to most people. Some people have called us 'the good folk,' but I'd say that's a misnomer if ever there was one."

"You seem to be an okay guy," Colin said.

Brogan smiled. "As I said, you're a good lad," the leprechaun replied as he stirred his tea. "But some would say your trust would be misplaced, since deception and mischief are in our very nature. A capricious lot we are, to the very last one of us. One moment we're helping you—the next, we're leading you off a cliff. It's only by outsmarting us that you'll have our help, in most cases." He nodded and sipped his tea. "No hard feelings about the alley, by the way. You caught me, fair and square. Now, where was I? Oh yes, I was telling you about when I was disturbed from my retirement, and when *he* showed up."

"And who is this 'he' you keep referring to? I take it he's the cause of all this?"

"*He* is the Avartagh, the foulest dwarf you ever did see. And, he's here to destroy every last thing you hold dear. Every. Last. Thing."

4

Colin continued munching on cookies, enrapt as Brogan continued his tale. "Years ago, good Fionn MacCumhaill defeated a terrible vampire dwarf known as the Avartagh, staking his heart and burying him upside down so he'd never return. But somehow, he found a way to escape his prison and follow me here."

"How'd he find you, Brogan? I mean, all the way from Scotland?"

Brogan scowled again. "Ireland, not Scotland. They really don't teach you much in school, do they?" Colin shrugged and nodded, since he thought school was mostly a waste of time. "In any case, he likely found what he was looking for by asking around among the remaining faery folk. A sad day it would be for the poor brownie or spriggan who was forced by the Avartagh to tell him what he wanted to know." Brogan shuddered visibly, and took a sip of tea. "Ah, that's the stuff. Barry's brand, hard to get over here—finally found it online."

Colin sipped his tea and found it much too strong and hot for his liking, so he stuffed a few macaroons in his mouth instead. "Whmmpph mmpphks thmmpph Avarmmphh suh bmmph?"

Brogan wiggled his eyebrows. "Good cookies, right? Love those macaroons, harder to get in Ireland than good Irish tea is to get here in the States." He took a sip and continued. "Well, to answer your question, what makes the Avartagh so bad is who he is. Are you familiar with the story of Vlad Tepes?"

"He's the real life version of Count Dracula, right? I wrote a report on him last year. He was the guy they based the Dracula story on, and he did some really gross stuff." Colin paused and shook his head in disbelief. "Wait a minute—you're telling me this Avartagh guy is a vampire?"

"Of sorts—and likely the first, actually. Many historians believe that modern vampire legends are based on the Avartagh. However, it's not blood he craves so much, but misery. And, whether the good people of your town are aware of it or not, he's preparing them for a huge heap of misery that he'll harvest and feast on for quite some time."

"But everyone seems so happy the way they are right now. I don't get it."

Brogan nodded and touched his finger to his nose. "Exactly! Think about how much of a shock that was to you earlier today, when you saw the town for what it's become over the last month or so. This morning, you were living your *dreams*. Everyone's local sports hero, spiffy motorbike, nearly perfect home life—how'd it feel to have it all yanked out from under you, all at once?"

Colin felt a pang of guilt, because for the first time in a month he could clearly remember his dad. And he felt the huge gaping hole his dad's absence had left his life. "Awful. I can hardly think of a worse feeling."

Brogan clapped a warm hand on his shoulder in sympathy. "Aye, me boy—I know. And had I never have come here, I wouldn't have played a part in your misery."

"But why, Brogan? I know you said most of the he-sh... fair folk are mean. But you seem pretty nice. Why would you do that?"

"And that's the billion-dollar question! Let me ask you, how much gold do you think a leprechaun of my age could amass over the centuries? Never mind, I'll answer that question for you, as it seems that the public school system isn't concerned with teaching you children to do maths in your head. The answer is, *a lot*. But just why do you think we do it? Obviously, we don't care to spend all that gold. My home is a nice place, but do you think it cost billions? Hardly."

"So what is the reason?" Colin's eyes lit up. "Wait a minute—a leprechaun's power is somehow connected to their gold?"

Brogan smiled like a school teacher proud of his favorite pupil. "In fact, not just power, but a leprechaun's life. A leprechaun is as connected to their gold as you are to the warm red stuff that flows in your veins. Without it, they'll wither away and die. A leprechaun needs his gold to survive."

"And the Avartagh stole yours—that's why you said you couldn't give me any gold if you wanted to."

Brogan smiled again. "Well now, me boy, I'm starting to think there's more to you than meets the eye. Got any Irish blood in you?"

"On my dad's side, yeah. But I have no idea how much. My dad passed away a few years ago, and my mom doesn't like to talk about him these days."

Brogan got a concerned look. "Far be it from me to bring up old wounds. But I have a feeling your father left you something important that may be the key to solving our mutual problem."

"I don't understand, Brogan."

"Well, it's not just anyone who can see through fairy magic. Remember the adder stone I mentioned? It's a special kind of rock with a natural hole in it that allows normal people to see through fairy magic and illusions. Granted, the Blarney stone triggered your release from the spell, but you must be *unique* for the stone to have reacted as it did. And for you to see me after? That's really something rare."

Colin sat back to take it all in while Brogan sipped his tea. "So what are you saying?"

"I'm saying that you may have the ability or resources to stop the Avartagh, and lift this spell so things can be set right again."

"But how?"

Brogan paused and looked up while tapping his chin. "I'm not sure exactly, but certainly there are forces at work here you don't yet understand. For one, what were the odds of you crashing your bike and flying into me at that exact moment? And, what are the chances it would happen with the one person in the whole town who can see me?"

"So, what you're saying is that this is fate?"

"Not fate. Something more. *Destiny*. And if I have my guesses right, it's your destiny to save this town and get rid of the Avartagh, once and for all."

"All I know is that I want to free my friends and my mom before they get hurt."

The leprechaun wore a grim expression as he replied. "And hurt they'll be if you don't find a way to stop the Avartagh. It's not just bad feelings he wants, but the desperation, desolation, and destruction of everyone in this town. Imagine the turmoil it will cause when the whole community suddenly discovers their dreams were nothing more than a ruse. The utter hopelessness will divide families, destroy lives, and tear this town apart. Just imagine what suffering it will cause when the Avartagh lifts the spell from the town."

"Then I need to find a way to stop him. And I'm going to need some help. What can you do to help me?"

"Not much, I'm afraid. I can do nothing against the Avartagh. I'm sure you can guess at the reasons behind my reluctance to do so."

"So why hasn't he lifted the spell already? It seems like he could have done it at any time."

The little man sighed, and slumped his shoulders a bit. "Because he wants to inflict the maximum pain he can, and the longer the good folk of this town live under this illusion, the worse it'll be when it lifts and they see it was all a dream. But the time is getting close, so now is the time to act."

"Well, if you can't help me then I'm going to have to recruit some help of my own. But right now everyone is under the spell of the Blarney stone, right? So how do I get anyone to help me?"

"Now that I can help you with." He handed Colin a small leather bag. "This is dust taken from the Blarney stone—'fairy dust,' if you will. Blow a pinch in the face of anyone under my spell, and they'll wake up immediately. Just make sure you do it somewhere safe."

"So they don't freak out when they see what's really going on."

"I say, you are a smart lad. By the way, Colin—what was your father's last name?"

"McCool. Why?"

A smile crossed Brogan's face that didn't quite reach his eyes. "I'd rather not say just yet. But trust me when I tell you, your part in these events is likely more important than you know."

5

As Colin was leaving Brogan's place, he suddenly remembered a very important detail that had been left out of their conversation. "Brogan, how do I find the Avartagh?"

"Oh, did I forget to mention that? He'll be easy to find, to be sure. He's pretending to be the mayor."

"You mean he's been posing as the mayor this whole time?"

"Since he arrived in this town. I suppose I should warn you about what you're up against, although admittedly your forebears might have dashed off to battle without asking the same."

"My fore-what?"

"Never mind. The Avartagh's powers include illusion and deception, although not on the level of a master druid. Even so, he can call upon numerous of the unseelie host to assist him, so expect fierce opposition in his allies. Also he's incredibly strong, fairly quick, and he'll play dirty, that's for certain."

"Great. What's an unseelie?"

Brogan sighed. "There's so much you don't know, and I wish I had more time to prepare you, but I believe time is short. Suffice it to say that the unseelie are the bad guys, although the lines tend to blur where Irish fae are concerned. In this case, you'll know them when you see them."

Colin nodded, started to say thanks again, but then caught himself at the last moment and instead held out his hand. "You've been a great help."

Brogan winked as he shook his hand. "You're a fast learner, me boy. I hazard to say that you'll prove to be of worth to me yet."

Colin climbed out of Brogan's manhole with a mission in mind. Brogan had told him that the best place to locate the Avartagh would be at the mayor's office, which seemed common-sense enough to him.

But first, he needed to get help—starting with Jesse. If he was lucky, they'd still be at the ball field, but he had to hurry.

As he jogged along back streets and alleys, he wondered if he should drop off his lucky bat at home and find a better weapon. He wished he had a sword, or a machine gun, or even a machete, but finally decided it was as good a weapon as he could find on short notice. Fact was that he'd never get rid of it anyway, since it was one of the last gifts he'd received from his father before he'd passed away.

Colin's dad had given him the bat on his eighth birthday, telling him it was a family heirloom. Despite the fact that it looked like an old, beat up ash bat, he still cherished it and took it with him to every game. Even before the spell had fallen over the town, he'd hit his first home run with it—a miracle in itself, since he'd never had much success in sports.

Once he picked his way out of the downtown area, he stuck to the alleys as he ran through familiar neighborhoods on his way to the ball field. Even from behind the houses he could see how weeks of neglect had taken a toll on the formerly beautiful neighborhoods where he and his friends had grown up. Trash littered the yards and streets, and neglected landscapes gave everything a slightly sinister appearance.

But the scariest things he saw were what others couldn't see. Several times since he'd left Brogan's manhole, he'd seen *things* roaming the streets and sidewalks of his town. Once, he saw a terrible white horse dripping with water and seaweed, and its breath looked like green mist blowing out of its nostrils and mouth. On another street, he saw some little men wearing red Santa Claus hats that dripped with blood. They carried long knives and cleavers, and played cruel tricks on the townsfolk. There were other creatures that, while not as frightening, still spooked him with their bizarre otherworldliness.

Colin simply acted as if he couldn't see any of them, because he suspected that if they knew he could, he'd be in a heap of trouble. He pulled his hoodie over his head and kept his eyes on the ground in front of him, only stealing glances here and there when he thought the creatures weren't looking.

He figured the quickest route was to take a shortcut through the park, since it'd save him considerable walking time and cut a good thirty minutes off his trip. As he neared the edge of town, the trees of the park appeared in the distance, but like the rest of the town they'd taken on a decidedly darker appearance since he'd touched Brogan's stone. The trees now seemed gnarled and twisted, and what he once considered to be a friendly and welcoming forest presently appeared to have sinister intentions. *Nothing to do but go through it*, he said to himself, remembering that he needed his best friend's help if he was to get back Brogan's gold.

As he entered the woods of the park, he noticed the light starting to dim. He looked up to see if the sun had been blocked by clouds, but instead saw tree limbs reaching for each other, almost as if they were trying to block out every last bit of sun. Colin shivered just a bit, then broke into a jog so he could make his time in this place as short as possible.

Coming around a bend in the path, he saw a patch of black and white fur from the corner of his vision. As he turned to look the way he'd come, nothing was visible; yet, he still knew that something had been back there, and possibly following him. He clutched his bat closer with both hands and continued jogging on.

Soon he heard movement in the woods, but the culprit remained concealed. Colin decided to pretend he didn't notice, but occasionally caught a flash of black fur in the trees several yards off the trail. Whatever it was, it moved with barely a sound, and yet every so often he could hear a rustle in the leaves, or a twig cracking. Finally, he decided that he was being trailed… or hunted.

He hurried along as his heart beat faster and faster, and the shadows grew longer the further he moved into the woods, even though it was barely after lunchtime. As he ran, the trail narrowed and tree limbs seemed to be reaching out to grab him—although he never actually saw them move. Twice he tripped over a tree root that he swore hadn't been there the moment before, and his face bled from scratches he'd suffered from errant tree limbs. Each time he fell, he picked himself up and ran as fast as he could manage toward the end of the trail.

Then, off in the distance behind him, he heard a terrible sound—like steam escaping a teapot—and the rapid clippity-clopping of a galloping horse. Looking over his shoulder, he spied a pitch black pony with eyes of yellow fire and chains clanking around its neck. It was moving fast, and from what he could tell the thing was bearing down on him as if to run him over. Colin's nerve left him and he made a break for it, veering off the trail in the hopes that he'd be able to avoid his pursuers by dodging through the trees.

As he turned off the trail, another tree branch tripped him and he fell into a thorn bush by the trailside. Landing in an awkward position, he could barely see the equine nightmare barreling toward him at a breakneck pace. At the last moment, he closed his eyes and covered his face with his bat and arms, in a futile attempt to protect himself from the horse's charge.

But instead of trampling him, the terrible beast leapt past him into the trees. When the horse landed, Colin heard the hiss of an alley cat preparing to fight, except it was much louder and lower. As he pulled himself out of the bush he saw the dark colt in a clearing, squaring off with the biggest cat he'd ever seen. The cat was pitch black, like the horse, except for a white blaze of fur on its chest.

Colin stood mesmerized, half-hiding behind a tree as his hands sought to crush the handle of his lucky bat. The cat arched its back and hissed once more, its eyes glowing yellow-green in the shadows. In response the colt danced and neighed, and it sounded like thunder and lightning all rolled into one to Colin's ears. The big feline arched its back again and pounced at the colt. Colin thought the horse was a goner, since the cat was nearly as large as the horse and had sharp claws and teeth.

But instead, the horse spun and lashed out with its rear hooves, and the cat was thrown across the clearing into a thick tree trunk. As the cat struggled back to its feet, the colt turned to Colin, and it spoke in a voice that seemed to come from nowhere and everywhere at once.

"Leave it to a fool human to stick around, when he should've been running. Hop on my back now, boy, if you want to make it out of these woods alive."

6

Colin hesitated, and the cat used the opportunity to leap around the fae colt and lunge at him. Purely based on instinct, he lashed out at the big cat with a backhanded stroke of his bat that caught the overgrown feline across the nose. Instead of the familiar *crack* he typically heard when making a home run or a nice line drive, it was more like the sound of a church bell tolling. *TOOOONNNNGG!!!*

Colin felt the impact all the way down the bat as the panther-like beast recoiled from the blow. It staggered back, shaking its head as though it'd run into a brick wall. The colt snorted in apparent amusement, then it pranced up to Colin and nudged him urgently with its forehead.

"Come now, we haven't much time. The cat sidhe hunt in pairs and this one's mate will not be far behind. Grab a handful of my mane and climb on so we can get you somewhere safer."

"But I've never ridden a horse—I'll fall off!"

The horse whinnied. *"You're obviously not familiar with the legends about my kind. Falling off is the least of your worries."* Then, the beast knelt down to allow him to easily climb on.

He took one glance at the huge black cat that was dizzily getting back to its feet and leapt up on the horse's back, gathering its mane in one hand and hanging onto his bat in the other. No sooner had he seated himself had the horse leapt to its hooves and galloped off, with Colin hanging on for dear life.

Colin had soon determined that leaning up against the colt's back was his best bet, since riding upright proved to be a painful lesson in avoiding tree limbs and stray branches. However, he also discovered that wherever his body came in contact with the creature's back, it stuck to it like glue. He even tried to readjust his hand grip, but found that he couldn't loosen his grip if he tried.

"Don't worry, it's not permanent. At least, not unless I want it to be.

We're almost there, so sit tight and I'll release you once we reach the edge of the woods."

"What are you?"

"A púca. I owed a favor to someone who knows you, and he sent me here to help."

"Was it Brogan?"

The horse shook its head. *"I don't know any Brogan. Someone else."*

Colin was quiet for a few moments, but then boredom got the best of him and he blurted out a question in order to break the silence. "So, where do you live?"

The horse looked back at Colin like he was crazy. *"In the bog."*

"Huh. So—what does a magic horse eat?"

The horse snorted, as if to express disapproval at the ridiculousness of the question. *"Mostly, young men who ask too many questions."* When Colin failed to speak again, the púca tossed his head as if he'd heard a funny joke. *"You have nothing to fear, for the moment. Normally I'd run into a swamp and drown you, then I'd feast on your carcass for several days. However, I've already eaten and haven't room left for dessert."*

Colin started at that last bit of information, and the horse whinnied again. *"Relax, boy, I'm no kelpie—I merely jest. In truth, I rarely take riders on my back. However, I do owe someone a favor, and that person seems to be looking out for your interests. Furthermore, after the blow you gave that cat with your shillelagh I'm not terribly inclined to cross you with that thing still in your hands."*

Despite the fact that it appeared the horse was merely having fun at his expense, Colin reflected that Brogan's advice not to trust any of the *aes sídhe* was the best advice he'd heard all week.

As they reached the edge of the woods, the púca came to an abrupt stop, kicking up the rich brown soil of the forest floor with its hooves. Although the beast had been running at a breakneck pace it was barely breathing, a fact Colin decided was altogether creepier than the horse's claims of eating people. He soon felt the strange magical stickiness of the horse's body and mane release, and he clumsily climbed off the colt and onto solid ground.

"I'd advise you to avoid these woods from now on. That cat sidhe is not likely to forget the blow you dealt her, and she and her mate are sure to hunt you should you ever come this way again."

"I'll keep that in mind. By the way, what's your name?"

The horse tossed its head and snorted in contempt. *"Has the old man taught you nothing yet? Names aren't freely given by the sidhe, boy, any fool knows that. For us, names are power, and it'd be the height of foolishness to give a human power over one of us."*

Colin nodded his head in reply. "I meant no offense, and I only wanted to remember the púca who'd been so helpful to me."

The horse whinnied and pawed the ground with its forehooves. "Well spoken. Apparently, you have been learning a thing or two about the sidhe after all. I keep my true name a secret, but you may call me Blackwillow if you must."

"Blackwillow, I'm Colin McCool. You've been a great help."

The horse tilted its head again slightly as if in approval. *"One last thing, boy—don't ever accept a ride from others of my kind, no matter what they tell you. It's sure to be your last if you do."*

Then, without another word, the colt turned and trotted quietly back into the woods. As Colin watched it disappear into the trees, he realized something the horse had said didn't make sense.

He cupped his hands to his mouth and called after the pony. "Blackwillow, wait! What old man?"

A high-pitched whinny in the distance was the púca's only reply.

"Well, the day keeps getting more mysterious as it goes along," Colin mumbled to himself as he got his bearings. "If I really have an Obi-wan, it'd sure be nice to know about it." Colin shook his head, then took off at a jog for the baseball field.

7

As Colin jogged to the top of the hill overlooking the field, he scanned the area for a sign of Jesse. The game had ended, but people still milled about the field and bleachers. As he approached he saw that the once bright yellow and white jerseys worn by his teammates were now threadbare rags that barely seemed serviceable. Trash and filth littered the bleachers, and the grass in the infield was almost as high as Colin's knees.

He finally spotted Jesse with her family, walking to an old beat up station wagon that must've been the real-life version of their new car. Colin was pretty sure that her dad's promotion and the money were all just a lie as well, like everything else in the town since the Avartagh had arrived. He knew she'd be devastated once he lifted the spell from her, but Colin desperately needed her help, and in all honesty he didn't want to face the Avartagh alone.

"Jesse!" he shouted from across the lot. She turned and waved, then said something to her parents and jogged over.

"Hey, if isn't our star player. What happened to you today? We could have used a few of your home runs. Anyway, I pitched a no-hitter so it's all good."

"Jesse, I really need to talk to you. It's urgent! Think you can ditch your parents?"

She glanced down at her ball and glove as a look of slight disappointment crossed her face. "Man, Mom and Dad were going to take me out to celebrate our win. You can come along if you want—Dad's treating, now that he's back to work again."

Colin didn't have the heart to tell her it was all a lie, but he still needed to free her from the spell so they could save the town. Yet he wasn't sure if that would make things better or worse than their current state. Despite the obvious poor condition of the town, everyone *seemed* to be much happier now than they were before. He wondered: would

Brogan lie to him just so he'd break the spell and cause even more grief and sadness?

Jesse snapped her fingers in front of his face. "Earth to Colin? Helllooo! You're doing that thing again, where you suck your thumb and try to make it look like you're not."

Colin shrugged off the thought and met Jesse's gaze. "It's nothing. Hey, do you think we could get a raincheck on burgers and shakes until later? I need your help with something and it just can't wait."

She sighed and punched Colin's shoulder. "I suppose I could be persuaded to help you. But you're going out with us tonight for sure. Deal?"

"Deal."

"Lemme go tell my parents."

Within a few moments, Jesse returned, and Colin led her over to the home team dugout. He grabbed her by the hand, and sat her down at one of the benches.

Jesse cocked her head and looked at him with a smirk on her face. "Colin, you are *not* going to ask me out, are you? I mean, we talked about this. No complicating our friendship—*that* was the deal."

This was a running joke between them, since everyone always assumed they were dating. On reflection, Colin concluded that it was kind of weird for a boy and girl to be best friends, but he really didn't care much what people thought.

Still, he dropped her hand like a hot rock and leaned back quickly. "No—I mean, it's not like that." Colin ran his hands through his hair and rubbed his face in frustration, concerned with what he was about to do to his best friend. "Look, I have something to show you, and it's in this bag right here—"

After Colin had lifted the spell on Jesse, she spent the next half-hour in a state of shock. At first she didn't believe Colin's story, so he challenged her to look outside the dugout. After she'd seen the sorry state of the baseball field and park, as well as the frightening appearance of the woods, Colin could tell she was beginning to accept the truth. However, what really convinced her was when he used the fairy stone

Brogan had given him to show her a goblin scampering around in the trash.

They sat together in the bleachers while Jesse wiped tears away from her eyes. "So it was all a lie? I mean, my dad's job and everything? He's going to be so disappointed when he finds out."

Colin rubbed her shoulder. "I know how hard it is, Jess. When I woke up from it earlier, I realized that for weeks I hadn't thought about my dad much at all. I almost wish I could go back to the way it was, so I didn't have to feel him gone all over again."

She sniffled and wiped her nose on a threadbare sleeve. "It's not just that—my mom and dad were having a lot of problems since Dad lost his job. They were fighting all the time, but things have been so good since Dad started working again. I'm worried it'll all fall apart once they know."

Colin rubbed his chin and shook his head. "Well, it's not all lost yet. Maybe there's a way to lift the spell and keep things the way they are—I mean, without all the trash and filth."

Jesse laughed as she wiped her eyes. "Yeah, it is pretty gross around here."

Colin waggled a finger at her. "You haven't seen anything, believe me. Wait till you see downtown."

Jesse got a serious look in her eye, and her face hardened for an instant. "All I know is, I want to find the sick puppy who did this to us, and make him pay."

Colin nodded in agreement, and he was glad to see that Jesse hadn't lost her knack for rolling with the punches. "I'm all for that. But just remember: Brogan says this dwarf is a scary guy. So, we'll have to be careful, no matter what we do."

Jess tilted her chin in the direction of town. "Well, what are we waiting for? Let's go kick some vampire dwarf butt."

8

Instead of short-cutting through the woods, they decided to "borrow" some bikes from the park. It seemed that people were leaving their belongings all over the place at random, so they happened across two bicycles in fairly decent shape lying in the grass. Since no one was around to claim them, they agreed to return them later after things had been straightened out.

Jesse yelled at Colin as they pedaled back into town. "Hey, let's stop off by your house and get something to eat—I'm starving."

"I guess it couldn't hurt to do this on a full stomach," he replied. They pedaled on and turned down Colin's street, and rolled up to the tall neglected grass of his front yard. As they got off their bikes, Colin noticed the front door was wide open. They heard a television blaring in the background.

"That's weird—Mom never leaves the doors unlocked or the TV on when she leaves." He grabbed his bat from the handlebars where he'd secured it and snuck into the front room of his house. Again, the neglect was apparent, as the floors were filthy and a horrible odor came from the kitchen.

Colin shut off the TV and called out to his mom. "Hey Mom, I'm home!" Silence.

Jesse stepped over some old pizza, and what looked like mildew in the carpet. "Dude, this place is gross. Now I know we've been under a spell, because your mom would never let your house get this nasty." She looked around and shrugged. "Think she's taking a nap?"

Colin glanced over at her and shook his head. "No, she never takes naps during the day. She says it's a waste of good sunlight. Let's check her studio and see if she's out there."

They walked through the kitchen, where the source of the smell became apparent. Trash and dirty dishes were stacked everywhere, and there were plates with old, maggoty food on the table. "Please tell me we weren't eating that," he mumbled to himself.

As they walked out the back door and crossed the driveway to the garage, they heard voices coming from that direction. Colin gestured to Jesse to stay hidden, and Jesse's eyes narrowed as she scowled in reply. He raised his hands and mouthed "sorry," creeping toward the garage. Jesse picked up a golf club from the driveway, holding it overhead like a samurai warrior as she followed him.

As they neared the garage door, the voices became more distinct, and there were sounds of things being thrown and moved around. Evil, high-pitched laughter alternated with mumbling and cursing, and there were three distinct voices amidst the ruckus.

The first voice they heard was deep and slow. "Hush! I think I hear someone coming."

Another voice responded that sounded like Jason Statham's evil older brother. "Nonsense, you plonker! 'Sides, no 'un can see us. So, keep lookin'—if we don't find what we came for, he'll skin us and eat us for dinner."

"Can we eat the woman? I'm tired of eating puppies and bunny rabbits—I want human meat!" This voice was whinier and more high-pitched than the other two. It reminded Colin of one of the Cobra Kai students from the original *Karate Kid* movie, the one who was always going, *"Yeah, Johnny, yeah—sweep the leg!"*

Evil Jason Statham responded. "Later, is what the Avartagh said. For now, we keep her safe until he says elsewise."

Weasel boy whined back, "Can't we just cut off some toes, or a hand for a snack? Just a bite?"

"Yeah," Deep-voice replied. "I'm hungry, too."

Colin and Jesse heard a loud *smack* and *thwap*, followed by the sounds of groaning.

"No!" Evil Jason Statham replied. "Do you really want to make him angry?" *Huh*, Colin thought. *Guess we know who the leader is in this bunch.*

Whiny-face sniffled a few times. "I guess not."

"Then keep looking for it, before the boy gets back."

Jesse tugged on Colin's arm, motioning for him to follow her around the side of the garage. She pointed at her eyes with two fingers, then into the window on the side of the building. They peered over the sill into the studio, spying three little men with red caps carrying long knives, pilfering Mrs. McCool's art supplies. The walls and floor were covered in paint, but Colin knew it was a leftover from his mom's Jackson Pollock phase.

They ducked back down before being discovered and leaned back against the wall. "Do you think they're talking about your mom? And what the heck are they looking for?"

Colin sucked the end of his thumb while clutching his bat tight. "I'm have no idea what they're looking for, but I'm about to find out what they did with my mom." He began to stand, but Jesse grabbed his arm and pulled him back down.

"Colin, stop! Are you sure that's a good idea? I mean, there's three of them that we can see, and only two of us. Besides, those things look pretty vicious. Maybe we can wait until they give up searching, and follow them back to where they're keeping your mom."

Colin sucked his thumb and took a deep breath. "You're probably right. But I want a backup plan, just in case we have to fight these guys. You stay here and keep an eye on them, and I'm going to sneak into the house to get some stuff that might come in handy."

Five minutes later, Colin returned with a backpack slung over his shoulder. He also threw some Twinkies to Jesse as he sat back down. "They last forever, thank goodness. Any movement in there?"

"I think they're about to give up. They've torn the place apart several times, and still they haven't found what they're looking for. What do you think they want?"

Colin's brow furrowed as he spoke. "I thought about it when I was inside, and I don't have a clue."

"Well, whatever it is, someone seems to want it pretty badly." She paused and looked down at his bat. "You think that's going to do much good against these things?"

He shrugged. "I don't know, but it seemed to come in handy back in the park. I think there must be something special about it that makes it hurt the *aes sidhe*."

"The what?"

"The 'ee-us-shee-thuh.'" He sounded out the words as if it would explain what it meant. "I can barely say it myself. Brogan said it's an old

Irish name for elves, sprites, leprechauns, and other fairy folk. He used the word to describe himself and the other creatures roaming around. From what Brogan told me, Irish fairies are sort of unpredictable. Some are downright evil, like those red caps in there, but even the nicer ones can't always be trusted."

Jesse squinted and pointed a finger in the air. "Uh, hello? That's something to think about, considering all of this started with that leprechaun, don't you think?"

"Yeah, the same thought crossed my mind. He owes me, though, and I don't think he can break his word once he's given it. So, until I get his gold back, I think we'll be able to trust him."

Jesse looked unconvinced, but shook her head and took another peek in the window. "Hey, I think they're leaving."

"Good. Let's go get our bikes and see if we can trail them without being seen."

9

Following at a discreet distance on their bikes, the red caps soon led them to the other side of the neighborhood. Here, the houses were separated from the rest of the town by a creek that ran through a culvert under the main road. The two ditched their bikes and snuck behind a hedge, from where they watched the red caps drop down into the culvert.

"Oh man, I am not following them in there!"

"C'mon, Jesse—we've been in there before."

"Yeah, but remember last time? That raccoon came out of nowhere and scared the daylights out of us."

"Jesse, we're chasing cannibalistic garden gnomes, and you're worried about a raccoon? Seriously?"

Jesse pinched Colin on the arm and twisted viciously. "Hey, raccoons are mean, and they *bite*." She made fangs with her fingers and rabbit teeth by biting her lower lip. Colin struggled to stay silent while his body shook with laughter.

Jesse rolled her eyes and threw her hands in the air. "Fine, be that way! I'll go in the stupid tunnel with the rabid raccoons and man-eating oompa-loompas. But you better have some flashlights in that backpack."

"Got 'em right here." He produced two flashlights and handed one to Jesse. "Look, you don't *have* to go in there with me."

"Hah! And let you to get eaten by the Keebler elves from hell? Uh-uh, no way I'm explaining that to your mom. Gimme a flashlight and let's do this."

Colin grinned smugly. "After you," he replied with a flourish of his arm and a mock bow.

"Yeah, 'ladies first'—look who's scared now." Jesse got down on her hands and knees and began crawling into the culvert.

"Well, if I'd have said I was going first because I'm the guy, you would have raised a stink. So, this is officially an equal opportunity suicide mission."

She stopped and looked back at Colin over her shoulder. "You are so getting it when we get out of here."

Colin shrugged. "What are friends for?"

About twenty-five feet into the tunnel Jesse stopped abruptly, which caused Colin to collide with her backside. He quickly backed off and pretended nothing had happened, but Jesse turned and scowled.

He gave a sheepish grin. "Sorry, I was trying to avoid looking at your, um, backside."

She cocked an eyebrow at him, which made him blush terribly. "Well, it appears you got an eyeful anyway, grace."

"Hey, this time I really was trying to be a gentleman!"

"Whatever, nerd." She leaned against the tunnel wall, gesturing toward an opening several feet ahead. "Anyway, it looks like they remodeled since we were here last. Shut off your flashlight and let me make sure no one is around." Jesse dropped to her belly and inched her way further into the tunnel, army-style. Colin saw a dim light ahead, but it was difficult to see much from where he was. Suddenly, Jesse disappeared from view.

"Jesse!" Colin whispered frantically. "Jesse!"

Jesse's head popped into view at the end of the tunnel and Colin jumped, banging his head on the roof of the culvert.

"Shush you big scaredy-cat, I'm right here. Now, get moving so we can find your mom."

"Ow!" Colin exclaimed as he rubbed his skull. "Man, you didn't have to scare me like that."

"Oh, yes I did. Bet you thought I was the raccoon."

He massaged his head as he clambered out of the tunnel and got to his feet. "I wasn't scared, just surprised. I knew it was you."

Jesse chuckled and punched Colin on the arm. "Big tough Colin. Now, what would you do without *me* to protect you from rabid raccoons and nasty red cap thingies?"

Colin had to admit, Jesse was the scrappier of the two. They'd actually become friends back in grade school. The day they'd met, Colin had been getting picked on for sucking his thumb, but on that particular day he'd had enough. He'd stood up to the kids who were bullying him, and ended up at the bottom of a dog pile getting pummeled. Jesse had saved him by beating kids off him with a plastic skateboard. They'd instantly become best friends, and although the teasing had eased up since, he was still glad to know she had his back.

"My hero," he replied with a smirk, and then turned on his flashlight and whistled. Somehow, the red caps had excavated a huge cavern directly beneath their neighborhood. Light was filtering down from a drainage grate above. "Wow, this place is ginormous—I hope this is still here after we get rid of these guys, because this would make a killer hideout."

Jesse nodded. "Sure beats the old treehouse in my backyard. Ugh, but what is that stench? It smells like old farts and rotten bacon."

"I'm not sure—maybe they busted into someone's sewer line or something. Anyway, let's figure out which way they went so we can find Mom." He saw three tunnels leading off from the room they'd entered. Colin searched the ground with his flashlight, looking for signs of where the red caps went. "Look, over here—these tracks look fresh."

Jesse patted him on the back. "I guess all those dorky scouting trips actually came in handy after all."

"Being an Eagle Scout is going to look good on my college applications. And besides, my dad wanted me to do scouting. It was sort of our thing."

Jesse's face fell. "Sorry, I didn't know it was something that you and your dad did."

"Hey, it's no big deal. Honestly, you probably didn't know because I don't like to talk about it much. I feel like I have to finish things I started with him, because it reminds me of when he was here."

Jesse put a hand on his shoulder and looked into his deep-set green eyes. "Hey, it's okay to miss him. He was your dad."

Colin looked away. "Yeah, but it makes me angry sometimes, and I get mad at him for leaving us. I mean, why did he have to go away to fight some dumb war? It didn't have anything to do with us, not really. Now he's gone, and all I have to remember him by are some stupid medals and a flag."

Jesse grabbed him gently by the chin and turned him to face her. "Colin, don't you think he believed in what he was doing? That it must have been important to him, if he did it even though he knew it would mean being away from you and your mom? I know I didn't spend a lot of time around your dad, but the times I did see you together it was clear he loved you."

"I know. I just wish he didn't leave us. And now that Mom might be missing—I couldn't take losing them both."

Jesse gave him a quick hug. "Don't worry, we'll find her." She stepped back, and handed him his bat. "C'mon, slugger. We have some red cap butt to kick."

Colin wiped his face on his sleeve, nodded, and headed off down the tunnel with Jesse in tow.

10

The tunnel they followed was much larger than the culvert pipe, and almost tall enough to stand up in the center. It had been excavated from the limestone bedrock common to the area, so they assumed it was fairly stable. Since it was apparently dug for the red caps, it wasn't quite man-sized, which meant they had to stay low as they followed it for a quarter-mile or more.

"How long do you think they were digging these tunnels?" Jesse asked.

"Hard to say, but with fairy magic involved I suppose there's no telling. Have you ever read any of the old fairy tales and stuff? They'd do things like take care of all the house cleaning and farm chores overnight for people, all for a saucer of milk. Or they'd spin straw into gold and other weird stuff. And trick people with magic." He paused for a second, and reached out to the wall, feeling it to see if it were real. "For all we know, this could all be another illusion."

Jesse knocked on the wall with her knuckles. "Feels pretty real to me. Hey, do you hear that?"

Colin cocked his head to listen. "Sounds like voices, and if I'm right that'll be the three stooges from Mom's studio." Motioning for Jesse to follow, Colin snuck further down the tunnel until he came to a bend. Peeking around the corner, he popped back and gestured for Jesse to back up a bit.

"It's them, alright—and they have my mom." A look of grim determination crossed his face. "I have a feeling that a golf club isn't going to do much against magical creatures with butcher knives and razor sharp teeth. You still go shooting with your dad?"

"Every Saturday, and Sundays when there's a three-gun event at the range. What's up?" Colin pulled a paintball gun out of his backpack. Jesse turned her nose up and scowled. "What, am I supposed to splat them to death?"

Colin shook his head. "Not with paint. This thing's loaded with OC powder, the same stuff they put in pepper spray. I found them with some of my dad's old gear, along with some smoke grenades. Plus, I hopped up the gun so it'd shoot harder and faster."

A wide grin crept across Jesse's face. "Some girls get diamonds, I get weapons of mass destruction. You are the man, Colin."

"Yeah, just make sure to hit them in the head if possible. It'll blind them and make it hard for them to breathe."

"How many paintballs do these things carry?" she asked.

"About 200, but you only have 50 shots or so."

Jesse nodded. "That's enough then. Double-taps to the head. That'll keep 'em down."

Colin chuckled. "Remind me not to make you mad, ever. Okay, here's the plan…"

Jesse and Colin soldier-crawled around the corner and hid behind some fallen rocks and debris. Colin's mom sat in a chair at an old kitchen table in the center of the cave. The red caps were busy preparing a meal over a fire in the corner—from the looks of it, the raccoon was going to be the main course. The pair heard the red caps arguing from across the cavern.

Whiny-face licked his lips. "Mmmmm… I want a drumstick."

Evil Jason Statham backhanded Whiny-face and sent him sprawling. "Idjit! Chickens have drumsticks, raccoons have haunches. Don'tcha ever watch Animal Planet?"

Whiny-face got up, pulled up a stool, and sat down. "Anyway, I still want a leg," he mumbled under his breath.

Evil Jason Statham reared back as if to strike again, and Whiny-face flinched. "You'll get what I give you. Now, what did the woman say?"

Deep-voice spoke up. "Nothing much. She says she doesn't know where the book is. Maybe the boy has it?"

"Idjits, both of you! Then we should've been out looking for him, instead of trashing the woman's home." They continued arguing back and forth, and Colin tuned them out.

"Okay, Jesse, when I give the signal, open fire."

"You're the mastermind of this little rescue operation," she replied.

Colin nodded, and raised his hand to count down. "Three—two—one—NOW!"

At Colin's signal, Jesse rolled out from behind the rubble and landed in a kneeling position. The paintball gun hissed, and screams of misery came from the red caps on the other side of the tunnel.

Whiny-face shouted as he hid his face. "Hornets! We're being attacked by hornets!" Jesse continued to lay down covering fire as Colin sprinted across the cave.

Evil Jason Statham was rolling on the floor rubbing his eyes with his palms, which was probably making it worse. "My eyes—they're burning! It's evil wizardry! The Avartagh has cursed us for not finding the book!"

The third red cap felt around blindly. "I can't see! I'm blind! Arrrggghhh!" He took off at a run and blasted straight into the wall, falling into a dazed heap on the floor.

Whiny-face was splashing soda in his eyes from a two-liter bottle, which fizzed and made his eyes look like they had rabies. "It burnssss usssss! Makes it stop!" he cried.

Colin grinned and popped a smoke grenade, then threw it in the red caps' direction. He rushed to the table where his mom sat and cut away the rope they'd used to tie her to the chair.

His mom's face lit up as he approached. "Colin! What a nice surprise. I was just about to have lunch with these pleasant young men. They're interested in my next art gallery opening, you know."

"Mom, I don't think those 'nice young men' are what they appear. C'mon, we have to go—now."

"But I've ordered roast duck!"

Colin glanced at the raccoon roasting on the fire and grimaced. "Mom, I wouldn't trust the chef. I believe he has hygiene issues."

Mrs. McCool covered her mouth in horror. "Oh, my. I must tell the waiter when he comes back."

"No time, Mom—we have to leave now because I'm double-parked."

His mother turned to him and shook a finger in his face. "Didn't I tell you not to get any more tickets?"

"Yeah, I don't think that's going to be a problem for a while.

Come on, we have to go!" He dragged his mother down the tunnel, heading back the way they came. Jesse took up the rear while laying down more covering fire, stinging the red caps with pepper balls as they ran into the walls, furniture, and other junk in the cave. One of them even set himself on fire in the confusion.

They hurried off down the tunnels, backtracking until they came to the room with the culvert pipe and three exits. As they entered the room, they saw a shadow moving in the culvert. Then two sets of glowing, feline eyes fixed on them and they heard a loud hiss.

"Oh no—it's the cat sith!"

Jesse shook her head. "I am *not* fighting Darth Vader, pepper paintball gun or no!"

"No, not that type of sith—but it's just as bad. Head back the way we came!" They ran back down the tunnel, but after a few steps they heard the red caps coming toward them yelling angrily.

"Gah! Back the other way," Jesse shouted. As they turned back, the two big cats jumped out of the culvert pipe. The cats hissed and spread out, attempting to flank them and cut off their escape.

Out of options, Colin pulled Jesse and his mom back into the tunnel again, slugging one of the red caps over the skull with his bat. The gnome stumbled into its brethren, tripping them to the floor of the tunnel.

There was a bright flash behind them in the direction of the cat sidhe. They turned around and saw the two panther-like creatures blinking and shaking their heads as if they'd been stunned.

"Shoot them!" Colin cried.

Jesse looked panicked. "I can't—it's jammed!"

Colin scanned the room in desperation to find the source of the bright flash, and saw a dark figure gesturing madly at them from one of the other tunnels. He grabbed his mom and yelled to Jesse, "This way!" and ran off after the retreating shape.

11

As Colin ran off down the tunnel after the fleeing figure, his mom chatted with Jesse as he dragged her along. "Now, Jesse, you really have to make it to one of my openings. You can come over to the house beforehand and we'll spend some time doing our hair and make it a girl's night. It'll be fun!"

"Not really in the mood to think about hair and makeup right now, Mrs. McC—I kind of have some other pressing issues here." She was fiddling with the paintball gun as she ran, trying to get it to fire again. After having no luck, Jesse tapped Colin on the shoulder. "Babe Ruth, you might be up to bat again soon. This gun is toast."

Mrs. McCool carried on, oblivious to the fact they were being chased by evil elves. "Oh, no worries, dear. I understand if you're bogged down right now with school and sports. We can take a raincheck on it."

Colin continued in pursuit of the mysterious figure, partially to escape, but also because he wanted answers. Blackwillow had hinted that someone was helping Colin behind the scenes, and with the apparent rescue they'd just received, Colin's curiosity was definitely piqued.

As he was rounding another bend in the tunnel, a head appeared out of the wall in front of him and stage-whispered, "In here!"

Colin skidded to a halt as the head disappeared back into the wall. "Ack! Did you see that?"

"See what?" Jesse responded. "I was trying to fix the paintball gun—what did I miss?" The head popped out of the wall again.

"I said 'in here' not 'wait out there to be eaten.' Are you daft?"

"Aaaagghh!" both Colin and Jesse screamed in unison, as two hands came out of the wall to drag Colin and Jesse in, with Mrs. McCool along with them. Once they passed through the wall, Colin saw they were actually in a small side tunnel off the main passageway they'd been running down.

In front of them stood the homeless man Colin had almost run into that morning. "You!" Colin shouted.

The old man put a finger to his lips and shushed him. "Quiet, fool! Those red caps may be bumbling idiots, but the cat sidhe are another matter. They are both crafty and expert hunters. So calm yourself until they pass."

The group stood quietly in awkward silence, staring alternately at the ground, the ceiling, their watches, and each other. After a minute or so, the man beckoned them to follow him down the small tunnel, speaking mostly to Colin as he led them farther in.

"This leads to a natural cave system that goes under most of your town. Those tunnels back there were dug by the local *buggane*. I hid this area with an illusion before they began to dig, and later connected the cave system with their tunnels so I could keep an eye on them."

"But who are you?" Colin asked as they hurried along behind him. "And, what do you have to do with the Avartagh?"

The old man led them into a small cavern that had obviously been adapted for use as a sleeping and living area. There was a cot in the corner, some bookshelves, and a desk and chair that was littered with old-fashioned documents, books, and maps. There were, however, several modern ballpoint pens and a spiral notebook among the older items. Colin also noticed an open can of Dr. Pepper on the desk as well.

The old man pulled up some stools and gestured for them to sit. "My name is Finnegas, although some call me 'Finn the Seer.' I've known your family for a very long time." As he spoke, his appearance subtly began to change. Where a scraggly old homeless person had rested a moment before now seated an equally thin, yet very proper-looking, older gentleman. Instead of the rags the homeless man had been wearing, he now dressed in corduroys, a dress shirt, and a tweed jacket.

Upon seeing his new appearance, Mrs. McCool perked up and peered at the old man through squinted eyes. "Uncle Finn, is that you?" Then, she leapt up and pulled him into a hug. "Where have you been? I haven't seen you since Colin's dad passed on."

Finnegas patted her back and gently pushed her away. "And it's nice to see you as well, Leanne." He took her hand and carefully guided her over to the cot, almost like a parent would with a child. "Now, lay down, lass, and take a nap." She did as she was told, and after she had lain down on the cot, he gently covered her eyes and mumbled something under his breath. Within moments, Mrs. McCool was in a deep sleep.

Finn gestured at Colin's mom with an ivory pipe that he'd pulled from his coat. "It's better if she sleeps, because her mind is in a fragile state. I've spent months waiting for the right sequence of events to present themselves so I could arrange for you to wake up from the spell. However, I fear that for some of the town, it may be too late to fully reverse the effects."

Colin stared at the old man, sucking his thumb absently. "Uncle Finn—hmmmm." Then, his eyes lit up. "I remember you! You used to take me fishing down at the pond in the park. I was just a little kid, and you would tell me fairy tales while we sat on the dock."

Finn puffed on his pipe, and smiled ruefully. "Those were better times. Better times for all."

Colin continued as more memories floated to the surface. "I remember—I remember a lady who used to swim in the pond. She'd float out in the water, and sing to us. She was beautiful, and her voice used to calm me down."

Finn gestured with his pipe again as smoke billowed around his head. "That woman was actually a water nymph. They can be nasty, but she seemed to be quite fond of you."

Colin rubbed his chin and gazed off in recollection. "When I was ten, I fell in the pond during the winter. I thought I was going to drown, but then someone pulled me out and I woke up on the dock."

"Yes, it was the nymph that saved you. As I said, she grew quite fond of you during the time we spent fishing her pond. In fact, I made certain to introduce you to several of the local Fair Folk that inhabit this area when you were a child, figuring that it may come in handy later when I was away. Turns out I was right."

12

Colin's mouth gaped, stunned as he was at the implications of what his memory and "Uncle Finn" were revealing to him.

Jesse took advantage of the lull in conversation to jump in. "Just a minute there, Gandalf—you're saying that a fairy saved Colin's life?"

The old man harrumphed at her characterization. "I'll have you know that Tolkien based that character on me, and not the other way around. We used to play chess every Tuesday, and he'd pester me about all sorts of strange creatures and lore. Why he felt he had to borrow from the Icelandic sagas, I'll never know."

Finnegas puffed on his pipe and blew smoke out of his nostrils. "Now, as for your question of whether or not a nymph is a fairy, they are, of a sort. But what most people today think of as fairies are a far cry from the Fair Folk that haunt the ancient places, both in the old country and where Europeans settled here in the New World."

Jesse arched an eyebrow at that. "So what you're saying is, these 'Fair Folk,' as you call them, have always been around—we just didn't or couldn't see them?"

"Both. Some people have the ability to see them; they just choose not to at an unconscious level." Finnegas took another moment to suck on his pipe again, puffing great clouds of fragrant pipe smoke as he continued. "Take Colin here as an example. As a child, he spent ample time with several of the local *aes sidhe*, interacting with them just as you and I are now. Yet, as he grew older, his mind somehow chose to filter out that information and those memories, and locked them away until he was forced to use them."

"You knew my dad." Colin gave the old man an accusing look. "I remember seeing you at his funeral."

Finnegas looked down as his hands cradled his pipe in his lap. "Yes, I did. And a finer warrior there never was in modern times. Your ancestors would have been proud."

"My 'ancestors'—Brogan said something similar to me earlier today. What do you mean by that?"

The old man tapped out the ashes from his pipe on his boot heel, then packed the pipe with more tobacco, tamped it down, and pointed at Colin with the mouthpiece of the pipe.

"You, young man, are from a long line of warriors, and have the blood of Fionn MacCumhaill himself in your veins."

"Finn McCool? I read about him last year, messing around in the library during study hall." Colin leaned forward, resting his chin on his fists as he soaked in all that Finnegas said.

"The very same. And though the legends say that Finn's *fianna* broke up once he passed on, it's not true. Or, rather, the *fianna* may have faded out for a bit, but those of your blood revived it in secrecy in later years. In fact, it was Finn's own son who revived it, the warrior-bard Oisín."

"It almost sounds as if you knew these people." Colin looked the old man in the eye and spoke it as an accusation.

"I did. Finn McCool was a student of mine, of sorts."

"That would make you thousands of years old," Jesse blurted out, covering her mouth after she spoke. "I hope that didn't sound rude."

Finn chuckled good-naturedly. "Not coming from as pretty a lass as you, my dear. And, you're right—I would be thousands of years old, if I hadn't lived most of the years since in *The Underrealms*, where the many of the *aes sidhe* still reside."

Colin spoke around his thumb as he answered. "But I thought once you went to the world of the fair folk, you had to stay there. Don't you age instantly when you come back to Earth?"

"No, not necessarily. I—have *ways* to circumvent the effects of visiting the youthful lands."

Colin nodded, grudgingly accepting the old man's story. "So how did you know my dad?"

Finnegas paused and leaned back in his chair, reflecting for a moment. "I owed your ancestor, Finn McCool, a great debt because of something he did for me. In honor of that debt, I agreed to look after the line of his male heirs, for as long as I am capable. I've been looking after your family for centuries, Colin."

"You said something about the 'fianna'—what is that?" Jesse asked. "It sounds like a girl's name, but you mentioned something about warriors."

Finnegas rocked back in his chair, crossed an ankle over a knee, and pointed at her with his pipe stem. "You don't miss a beat, do you, lass?" He tilted his head at her in appreciation and continued. "The fianna were young warriors of no small skill and fame in old Ireland. They were protectors of the lands, and helped keep the peace in those times. But after Finn fell to treachery, his son O'Sheen revived the true fianna in secret. Since that time, the McCool line has been responsible for carrying on the tradition, banding together with other warriors to protect those in need."

Colin's face fell like a stone. "That's why my dad was a soldier. He went to war to protect people."

"He went to war because he believed it was right. But also, for other reasons I'd rather not speak about at this time. Your father was a good man, a proud warrior, and a true hero. And he loved you and your mother very, very much."

"So what does this have to do with me?"

"For that answer, we have to go back to when Finn McCool was called on to slay the Avartagh. Some legends give credit for that noteworthy deed to the war chieftain Cathrain, but in truth it was Finn who finally put that foul thing to rest. Cathrain killed him, but the evil dwarf kept coming back. Finally, he called on McCool for his help, and Finn put it down for good—with a little help."

Colin rubbed his chin absently with a wet thumb. "But if Finn put him down for good, how is it that the Avartagh is back now?"

"Well, the Avartagh can't truly be killed, since he is one of the *neamh-mhairbh*, or undead. The only way to stop him is to pierce his heart with a yew wood sword to weaken him, and then bury him upside down under a large stone so he can't escape by clawing his way out. Unfortunately, several years back he was set free, in a construction accident that I tried to prevent. The ground where the Avartagh was buried was soaked in blood, which revived him. When the workers removed his burial stone, it allowed him to struggle free. And here he is."

"But what does he want?" Colin asked.

"For starters, he wants to see the line of Finn McCool ended. But he believes you have something he desperately wants, which is why he hasn't killed you yet."

13

Colin's eyes narrowed as he replied. "Let me guess—he's looking for a book."

"Yes, your father's journal. It was one of your father's possessions, to be passed on to you when you come of age. He'll never find it, though, as I've hidden it away for safe-keeping—until you're ready for it."

Jesse raised her hand and spoke up. "Excuse me for butting in, but why the heck does this evil dwarf want Colin's dad's journal?"

"Good question. You see, it's much more than just a journal. In fact, it's a tome of the collected battle wisdom of the McCool clan over multiple generations. In truth, it's more of an encyclopedia than a book per se. Although I haven't determined why yet, it obviously contains information he needs."

The old man turned and gestured toward the object in Colin's hand. "You know, your father also left you something that'll prove much more useful in your present situation."

"My bat? Yeah, it's come in handy more than once today."

Finnegas nodded. "As you've already seen, that 'bat' is a lot more than it appears. Can I see it for a moment?"

"Sure." Colin handed it over to him, handle first.

"Watch what happens when I cancel the glamour that hides its true appearance." Finn spoke a few words in a language that Colin didn't recognize, and the bat was transformed into a war club, banded with a dull grey metal at the end, and with a grotesque face carved into the handle at the butt.

"Wow—that's what I've been carrying all this time? Wicked." Colin grinned from ear-to-ear.

Jesse chimed in with a whistle. "No wonder you've been hitting all those home runs."

"Indeed," Finnegas said. "With this club, you could make it to the majors before you hit college age, I'm sure. Although, you might get into trouble eventually for shredding baseballs. It packs quite a wallop, as you've seen."

"All I know is that even Blackwillow was afraid of it—or, at least, he gave it a healthy respect."

"Creatures like Blackwillow know what your war club was made for, which is specifically for smashing *sidhe* skulls. Very few fae could stand against it in battle. It was actually a gift from Ogma to your ancestor many centuries ago."

"Ogma—isn't he like a war god?"

"Yes and no. Ogma was one of the tuatha deities, and a great warrior. People mistook them for gods, but they were—something else. Not really gods, but powerful and strange enough to fool most folk. Ogma was known for carrying a great war club, which he used quite effectively in battle. I suspect your father left the club to you because he knew you'd need it someday."

Colin rubbed his hands over his face and through his shaggy red-brown hair, and then then looked up at Finnegas with a grim expression. "Enough talk. Now, how do we kill this thing and put it in the ground, for good?"

They followed Finnegas down a long cave corridor that seemed to run parallel to the tunnels where they'd left the cat sith and red caps. "Now, remember, in order to stop the Avartagh you need to pierce him with a yew shaft. Can either of you shoot a bow or crossbow, or throw a javelin?"

"Jesse's pretty good with a gun—real good, actually." Colin turned to face his friend. "I don't want to ask you to do anything you don't want to do, but I don't think I can do this alone."

She punched him in the shoulder teasingly. "C'mon, you think I'm going to let you have all the fun? Despite the fact that my dad doesn't actually have his job back, and that we're probably going to be in the poor house again soon, this is the most fun we've had since we threw dry ice and red food coloring in the school pool last Halloween. I'm in."

Finnegas nodded approvingly at the two. "And so it begins. Frankly, I've been itching to see another female warrior in the fianna, as we haven't had one for decades." He motioned them to follow as he entered a side room off the tunnel they'd been traveling. As they entered and their flashlights illuminated the room, they could see a wide variety of weapons and armor, including spears and javelins, swords, clubs and maces, and an assortment of bows and crossbows.

Finnegas rummaged around for a bit, and then produced a small, hand-held crossbow and a brace of bolts. "Here, girl, this should serve you nicely. It's small but powerful—enchanted, you see. The bolts are made of yew, with a nasty little surprise on the tips as well. Careful not to nick yourself with them." He handed them over, and Jesse looked the weapons over appraisingly.

"Don't we get any armor?" Colin asked. "I mean, it seems like it might help, considering that we're going up against a crazy undead vampire dwarf."

Jesse chimed in. "Undead vampire is redundant. Besides that, if he's undead, then how do we kill him?"

"You can't kill him; you can only stop him. The yew arrows will weaken him, but Colin will have to do most of the hard work. And, I'm afraid that without training, armor will just slow you down."

Colin threw his hands up in protest. "You mean I don't even get a shield? This blows!"

Finnegas rubbed his chin as he looked up at the ceiling. "Hmmmm—well I suppose I could find something around here." He rummaged around in the piles of weapons and armor that littered the area. "Ah-hah! Here we are, just the thing for you." He stood back up and produced a small shield approximately the size of a dinner plate.

Colin looked like he'd been slapped. "You have got to be kidding me. I'm going up against one of the scariest guys Finn McCool ever faced, and you're sending me in with a pie tin and a bat?"

"Ah, but not just any 'pie tin'—this buckler belonged to one of your ancestors, who carried it in battle against a mighty buggane, which he slew. It's enchanted to help the wielder block more quickly and accurately. Better than any shield five times its size—and it won't slow you down, either."

Colin reluctantly took the small shield. "Okay, so what's the plan?"

"Simple, really. The lass will shoot the Avartagh full of crossbow bolts, and you'll come in after and pummel him into little mushy bits with your club. Then, we'll put him in a box lined with silver, and bury him upside down in about five tons of concrete."

"Concrete? I thought you said he had to be buried under a rock?"

"Well, for some things only ancient technology and magic will do, but personally I think modern science holds the trump card where vampire burials are concerned. Nothing says 'stay put for all eternity' like a few tons of steel reinforced concrete."

Colin shook his head, still unconvinced. "Well, it didn't keep that fat vampire on *True Blood* down, but I suppose you're the expert. So, where do we find this thing?"

14

According to Finnegas, the Avartagh was using city hall as his headquarters. The plan was that Finnegas would lead them through the tunnels where they connected with the city hall subbasement. From there, they would sneak into the building, locate the Avartagh, and dispatch him in due haste.

Jesse raised her hand. "Hey, quick question for you, Finnegas—how am I supposed to shoot this thing and hold that fairy stone to my eye at the same time?"

"Well, let me ask you this—did you have any issues seeing the red caps or cat sith when they were chasing you through the tunnels?"

"Come to think of it—no, I didn't. So why did I have to look through the thing the first time at the park?"

Finnegas raised a finger as if to make a point. "That's just what I was referring to earlier. Some people have a *natural* ability to see what others don't, but most choose to block that information out. Sometimes all it takes is seeing what's really there a time or two to jump start your brain back into 'remembering' how to see the world beneath our own."

Jesse tilted her head and nodded. "So I should be able to see the Avartagh and other fair folk now. Sounds reasonable to me—at least, as reasonable as the idea of seeing fairies and vampire dwarves can be."

Finnegas led them further down the cave tunnels to an opening that connected with the city sewer system. "Now, this entrance to the sewers is also hidden by magic, but once you leave this tunnel you'll be exposed to the Avartagh's cronies again. There's a ladder straight ahead that connects with the maintenance tunnels under City Hall. I suggest you head directly to the mayor's office and dispose of him quickly, before he can summon any other *sidhe* to his aid."

"You're not coming with us?" Colin exclaimed. "Oh, come on. You're the one with magical powers—how come you're not helping to kill this thing?"

"Quite simply, because I have other important things to do, and

I'm the only one who can do them. Once you 'kill' the Avartagh, the spell should be broken, at which time all the local citizens will come to and realize that everything they've seen and done for the past few weeks was an illusion. I'll have to cast another spell to convince them that all the damage to the town was the cause of some natural disaster."

Jesse arched an eyebrow at the old man, who shrugged. "It's thin, I know," he said, "but it'll have to do."

Finnegas saw the worried look on Jesse's face, and patted her gently on the arm. "Now, now, lass—everything will be fine. I know you're worried about your father's job, but I'm sure it will all work out." He turned to Colin then, grabbing him gently by the shoulders and looking in the eye. "Hear me, boy: you *can* do this! I know you doubt yourself, because it's written all over your face. But trust me, you have the blood of generations of warriors running in your veins—you were born for battles such as this one."

Colin perked up at that. "Any last words of advice?"

Finnegas touched his index finger to his chin, and looked thoughtful for a moment. "I suppose I should tell you what you'll be facing. The Avartagh is crafty and he has the power to disguise himself, which is how he was able to fool everyone when he first arrived. He is also quite strong and quick, although he prefers to use trickery to defeat his opponents, instead of sheer strength. Oh, and he bites, so don't expect a fair fight."

"Sounds tough. I suppose I have some sort of super-warrior powers that I can break out at just the right time to defeat the Avartagh. Am I right?"

Finnegas started laughing, and laughed so hard he bent over in two and slapped his thighs. "Oh, that's a good one, boy." He wheezed out a few more belly laughs, and wiped his eyes. "Ah, you're a funny one, but you watch too much television. No, you won't manifest 'super powers'—at least not at your age. The fianna train for years to learn how to channel their talents, and you haven't even started your training yet. No, you'll have to defeat the Avartagh on surprise and luck alone—well, and that club you're carrying."

Colin rolled his eyes. "Great, some motivational speaker you've turned out to be." He turned to Jesse and motioned her to follow. "C'mon, Jesse. Let's go get this over with."

Jesse gave the old man a mean look and whispered under her breath as she passed. "You could have just lied to him, you know."

The old man managed to look mildly offended. "What, and give him false hope? There's enough of that in the world these days, I can tell you that. No, he needs to go into battle knowing that he wins or dies today based on his own will and wits."

Colin put his fingers in his ears. "LA-LA-LA-LA-LA! I'm not listening to you right now! LA-LA-LA-LA-LA!"

Jesse pushed him out of the tunnel. "Oh, let's go, you big baby. I mean, how tough can a three-foot tall vampire be?"

15

They had no trouble finding the entrance to the maintenance tunnels below City Hall. Once they were in, they found the exit to the building and took a peek down the hallway. "I seem to remember that the mayor's office is on the top floor," Jesse said. "That means we'll have to sneak past *them*."

Colin peered over her shoulder to see what she was referring to. "All I see are a bunch of cheerleaders. They're kind of cute, but they don't look so tough."

"Um, Colin? Look at their feet. Somebody seriously needs a pedicure."

Colin looked down, and at first all he saw were normal feet in regular old tennis shoes. But, something was off about the way the cheerleaders were walking. He blinked, and then he saw that instead of human legs and feet, the girls had goat's legs and hooves.

"Ugh, that's gross! I'm going to have nightmares about this for weeks."

"Yeah, well don't sweat it, slugger—I think those girls are out of your league, anyway. For one, they look varsity squad to me, and second—oh crud, one of them saw me!"

One of the cheerleaders shook a pom-pom covered fist directly at Colin and smiled a wicked smile at him. "There you are! We've been expecting you." Dance music with a strong bass line started playing, and the girls began doing a cheer routine in the hallway. *"Colin, Colin, he's our man, come on over, yes you can!"*

Colin's eyes glazed over, and his club slipped out of his fingers as he began walking toward the unseelie cheer squad. A goofy smile spread across his face, and he plodded slowly down the hallway.

Jesse stepped out in front of him, snapping her fingers in front of his face. "Colin, snap out of it!" She slapped him, at first lightly, and then hard across the face, to no effect. Then, she turned and fired a crossbow bolt at the head cheerleader, but the girl deftly batted it aside as she cart-wheeled in front of her squad.

Jesse turned to face Colin again and tried to push him back down the hall. Unfortunately, he was too strong for her, and continued his slow march toward certain doom. Throwing her hands up in the air, Jesse reached up, grabbed Colin on each side of his face, and kissed him, right on the mouth. She stayed there for a moment, until Colin's eyes turned inward to focus on her lips, plastered to his own.

"Mrrrph!" was all he could manage to say. Jesse backed off, breathing heavily, while Colin stood in stunned silence.

She cocked her hip against her right hand, and tossed her hair back, pointing down the hall with her other hand. "You can thank me later. Now, would you please go kick some cheerleader butt?"

Colin blinked his eyes rapidly, then turned to pick up his bat. "Uh, sure thing. Um, yeah – getting right on that." He walked past Jesse a few steps, then turned back to her, shook his head, and ran after the cheerleaders. He had no words for what had just taken place.

Jesse bit her lip and sighed. "Aw, man, I hope this doesn't complicate things," she mumbled, under her breath.

Once the cheerleaders saw their spell was broken they scattered to the four directions, wanting no part of Colin and his war club. After watching the fae cheer squad flee, Jesse and Colin found the stairwell that led up to the executive offices.

Colin chuckled and nudged his best friend playfully. "That was quick thinking, back there. Um, thanks?"

Jesse looked down at her crossbow, failing to make eye contact with him. "Yeah, well—I didn't want you to get eaten by the psycho cheerleaders from hell. I don't know if you noticed, but that one in front had a seriously messed up grill. It looked like she might have been taking vampire lessons from this Avartagh character."

Colin grinned. "Well—thanks. I owe you one."

She smiled and nudged him back, hard enough to push him into the wall. "You owe me *tons*. And don't forget it."

"I won't—but you know this breaks our agreement, right?"

Jesse threw her hands up in the air in frustration. "Argh! I knew you were going to make this weird." She stomped off up the stairs, taking them two at a time.

"Jesse, wait! What did I say? I'm just kidding—honest!" As she ducked around the corner out of sight, he sighed and took off at a run after her. He caught up with her as she reached the second floor landing, and pulled up behind her as she stopped dead in her tracks. "Why are you stopping?"

"I think we have a problem, slugger. You're up to bat."

Colin looked around her and saw what she was referring to—it was the red caps from his house and the tunnels, and they looked pretty hacked.

One of them began licking his lips. His teeth were coated in yellow-green filth. Their hats looked wet, as if they'd been recently soaked in dye… or blood. "Finally, a decent meal. I call dibs on the girl's drumsticks."

Their leader slapped the one who spoke up. "Silence! I called dibs already. And besides, there's plenty to go around. So long as we get them to tell us where the book is, the Avartagh says we can do with them as we want."

Jesse started to go after the red caps, but Colin held her back. She shook a finger at them while she strained to get past Colin's arm. "Now look here: first off, no one is having my 'drumsticks,' and second, we're not telling you squat!"

Colin stage whispered to her. "You can start shooting these guys at any time now."

Jesse stage whispered back, "Oh, yeah—I forgot I was holding this thing." She shot the one that had called dibs on eating her, right between the eyes. The thing toppled backward, kicked its foot a few times, then went still.

As the other red caps looked on in shock at the fate of their former partner in crime, Colin leapt forward with a war whoop and batted them both into the wall, where they crumpled in a heap of splayed arms and legs. He chuckled to himself.

"Nice shot," he told Jesse.

"Nice swing," she replied. "Ready to go take on the mayor?"

"Ready when you are, but I have a sneaking suspicion he knows we're coming. So, as soon as you see him, shoot him—alright?"

"You got it, chief." Colin pushed open the door to the second floor, and Jesse followed him through.

16

As they exited the stairwell, there were elevators to their left, and a frosted glass door that said "Mayor's Office" directly in front of them. Colin pushed through the door with Jesse not far behind.

Having decided the time for subterfuge was over, he walked boldly down the center of the hallway with his bat held over his shoulders, one hand resting on each end. Jesse took up the rear, crossbow reloaded with a bolt at the ready. They approached a reception area that was backed by a wall, with two entrances on either side. The wall obscured the view beyond, so Jesse tapped Colin on the shoulder to get his attention.

"You go left, and I go right?" she suggested. Colin nodded, and they positioned themselves with their backs to the wall at the corners of the entryways. Colin silently counted with his fingers to three, and on three they both burst around the corners of the wall, ready for whatever might pop out at them.

Fortunately for them, nothing waited to jump them here. The second floor of City Hall housing the mayor's office was deserted, and the desks and chairs that littered the long open work area before them appeared to have been disused and abandoned for weeks.

"Wow, I guess not much work has been getting done in the mayor's office recently," Colin said.

"According to my dad, that'd be business as usual," replied Jesse. "Since the recession hit, he's not too keen on politics in general and politicians in particular."

"Well, now that I know the mayor is actually a vicious, blood-sucking dwarf, I'm not so keen on politicians, either." Colin picked his way through the mess as he walked toward the large frosted glass door at the end of the room labeled "John Boynton, Mayor."

As they approached the door it slowly creaked open, and there was the mayor sitting behind his desk, staring at them with a blank-eyed expression.

"Shoot him!" Colin cried.

"But he's just sitting there—I don't see any red glowing eyes or fangs!"

"It's a trick! Just shoot him already!"

Jesse hesitated, then raised her crossbow. "Oh, alright," she replied, and with a *twang* a crossbow bolt appeared in the mayor's right shoulder. He slumped down in the chair and out of sight behind the desk.

"Well, that was easy," Colin stated.

Jesse waved him forward with her free hand. "Go make sure he's out of commission before he gets back up!"

Colin entered the mayor's office and slowly tiptoed around his huge mahogany desk with his club and shield at the ready. As he peeked around the mayor's desk, a confused expression crossed his face. "He's out cold. Huh. I'd expected more of a fight from him than that." He waited for a reply from Jesse, but instead heard nothing but silence.

"Jesse, I said he's out cold." All he heard in response was silence.

Colin peeked up over the desk, and saw his friend walking toward him from the reception area. At first she looked angry, for some reason. Then she smirked and made a 'hurry up' motion with her hand. "Well, if he's out cold it's our lucky day—finish him off!"

"I don't know—it looks like he's out of it, and to tell the truth, he seems pretty harmless." Colin looked at the mayor again, and doubt began to settle in his gut. He turned back to his friend to gauge her response.

Jesse frowned and shook her head. "You don't know that, Colin. It could just be the yew crossbow bolt that knocked him out. Didn't Finnegas tell you something about it weakening him? He might wake up at any moment and kill us both. I know it seems cruel, but you have to do it."

Colin looked at the mayor. "I don't know Jess. It just seems *wrong* somehow."

She looked a bit more irritated this time at his insistence that they spare the mayor. "Of course it seems wrong, because he looks like the mayor. But he's not! And, if you want to save the town, us, your mom, and everyone else who lives here, you have to kill him. Now!"

"Maybe I could just tie him up—"

Jesse's voice got two octaves deeper and a whole lot louder as she replied. "I said, *finish him off!*"

Colin wasn't sure what to make of his friend and ally, the girl who had saved him from bullies and playground tyrants more times than he cared to count.

"Jesse, are you okay? You don't look so good—in fact, you don't sound so good either. Maybe you should just sit down while I tie Mr. Fake Mayor here up."

Then, he looked more closely at his friend... and that's when Colin realized that Jesse wasn't Jesse at all.

17

Jesse threw her hands up in the air in exasperation. Her voice took on an even deeper timber as she spoke. "Argh! By the burning eye of Balor—do I have to do everything myself?"

At that moment, her eyes rolled back in her head and the whites of her eyes turned red as the fluorescent lights overhead began to flicker. Her eyelids and eye sockets began to bruise and darken, her skin became so pale it was nearly transparent, and veins popped out on her forehead and arms. Her hair began billowing around her face, although there was no breeze in the building.

Colin shook his head in disbelief. "You're not Jesse."

She replied in a deep, maniacal voice. "And what gave you that idea—boy?"

Not-Jesse spat the last word out as an accusation, and to Colin it seemed to carry all the hatred and venom of a decade of playground and schoolyard teasing and taunting.

"I search halfway around the world to find the heir of Finn McCool to take my revenge on his progeny, and all I find is a scared, pudgy whelp who sucks him thumb. Imagine my disappointment." The not-Jesse thing looked at him and *tsked* in a mockery of pity.

Colin was angry, but frightened as well, and felt as if he might bolt at any moment. It was an unnatural fear, almost overwhelming at times. But soon he realized the fear wasn't coming from him, but instead from the not-Jesse *thing* in front of him. He clutched his bat in both hands, still hesitant to strike his best friend should she turn out to be herself and under the influence of the Avartagh. He steeled his courage and spoke.

"What did you do with Jesse?"

"Are you worried about your friend—or perhaps merely frightened that she's not here to save you? Poor, little Colin. How you shame your ancestors. You're nothing more than a fat, scared boy who is still frightened to be alone, such a far cry from the warriors who once stood against me and my kind."

Not-Jesse examined her nails while she feigned boredom and sighed. "Since it appears I won't be able to frame you and your friend for the murder of the mayor, the least I can do is take her away from you—and sadly, there's nothing you can do about it."

Colin's hands turned white as they gripped his war club tightly at waist level. He hissed out the words as they escaped his gritted teeth. "Where—is—Jesse?"

Not-Jesse laughed and tossed her hair back. "Oh, she's here *somewhere*—and I'm sure she's having a splendid time with my *baobhan sidhe*, whom you've already met. You see, they don't like to lose their prey, and when she spoiled all their fun they decided they didn't like her very much. And although they're partial to young men, they shouldn't have much trouble draining her pretty veins dry before we're finished here. So, I can *still* kill the mayor and make it look like it was you." Not-Jesse looked thoughtful for a moment. "I suppose I can even pin Jesse's death on you, too."

Colin screamed, and it was a primal sound that drove up from his gut, through his lungs, and out his mouth like the roar of a lion. He charged the not-Jesse thing and swung with all his might, only to have her disappear like a wisp of smoke as his club passed harmlessly through empty space.

He heard a wicked laugh from behind, and then he was struck violently across the arm and shoulder. The impact tossed him like a rag doll, across the room and into a desk and chair. As Colin landed he lost his grip on the war club, and it went clattering across the floor. He lay there stunned for a moment, then struggled to get up as he looked to see where the evil not-Jesse had gone. It only took a moment to spot her advancing on him from across the room. She'd take a slow step, then she would blur and move several feet toward him in an instant, just like in his dream.

Colin was petrified, because without his club he had no means of protecting himself. Then he remembered the shield Finnegas gave him, and fumbled around in his backpack for it. No sooner had he got it on his arm had the thing that wasn't Jesse appeared in front of him.

Not-Jesse immediately began hammering him with blows that felt like jackhammers, and he was barely able to block them all with the little shield.

The thing's face was sculpted in hate, and it shouted angrily with words that punctuated each blow.

"For centuries I rotted in the ground, all due in no small part to your ancestor, that treacherous Fionn MacCumhaill! Then, I emerge to find a world where the Fair Folk are no longer feared and respected, where people use machines instead of magic, and where the line of McCool has abandoned the Isles and escaped to the New World. But I had vowed revenge, and revenge I'll have, even if it's on the miserable little shadow of a MacCumhaill that stands before me."

Finally, Colin managed to get some space and rolled away from the Avartagh. He was bleeding from a split lip, had at least one loose tooth, and was having a hard time hearing from his right ear. Colin doubted he could withstand another attack like that, and searched the room for his club. Looking around frantically, he saw his bat was on the other side of the room from him, directly opposite and behind the ghoulish imitation of Jesse that stood in his way.

The Avartagh advanced on him menacingly. With each step, the creature thrust a clawed finger at him, punctuating his words. "You, boy—you will be the last of Fionn MacCumhaill's line to walk this earth. And if I have any say in it, you'll go down in history as a murderer, not a hero. I'll sully the name 'McCool' forever, as I end your miserable existence for all time."

The Avartagh's eyes were glowing now, in a sick deep red that resembled the color of clotted blood. Colin watched as claws formed at the end of its fingers, and the vampire's teeth lengthened considerably. Each tooth grew into wicked little points that reminded Colin of an evil clown mask he'd worn one Halloween.

After the Avartagh's transformation was complete, he sprang forward in a blur and landed a punishing blow against the little shield Colin held. It cracked it down the middle and Colin flew back into the mayor's office, where he bounced off the metal frame of the plate glass windows and fell behind the mayor's desk.

Colin pulled himself to a sitting position against the wall, wincing at the pain in his side and back. He was having difficulty breathing, and with every breath he felt bones grinding in his chest. Blood flowed profusely from his forehead, and he could barely lift the arm from which the broken shield pieces dangled.

He looked over at the mayor, and thankfully he could see the mayor's chest rising and falling gently. Then he looked up to see the Avartagh floating toward him. As it did, the creature morphed again, from a twisted caricature of his best friend into an equally ghoulish version of the leprechaun, Brogan.

Colin harrumphed and spat out a mouthful of blood on the floor beside him. "So, you're the Avartagh. Somehow, I knew I couldn't trust you—I just didn't know why exactly."

The Avartagh laughed and floated to land on top of the desk, where it leaned on one knee and stared menacingly at Colin. "And now you've finally realized the very nature of the so-called 'fair folk'—that not one of us can ever be trusted. I warned you myself, did I not? But then again, none of you fools ever listen—at least, not until it's too late." The creature grinned a wicked grin and chuckled softly.

"Imagine, boy: imagine all the heartache and pain that will be caused when the spell is lifted from this town! Imagine the misery! Families will split apart, lives will be ruined, and I'll be beneath it all, feasting on the misery for years and years to come. Do you know how sweet the blood is from someone who has no hope? When I drain their veins in their homes at night, they'll be begging for me to take their lives—and I'll savor every last drop. And the best part is, I'll be able to feed on all their misery for decades to come."

Colin made a half-hearted attempt to pick himself up, but then seemed to lose his balance and slump off to the side. The Avartagh laughed at him.

"Don't die on me yet, boy! I want you to watch me beat the mayor bloody with your own shillelagh. Then, I'll make it look as though he fought valiantly against you, wounding you fatally as he died from the beating you gave him. Imagine the grief on your mother's face, when she finds out her boy was a cold-blooded murderer. After losing her husband, I'm certain the strain will be much more than she can bear."

18

"No!" Colin screamed, as he lunged up from behind the desk with a bloody crossbow bolt in his hand, ripped from the shoulder of the mayor. He plunged it deep into the chest of the Avartagh, then without hesitating or waiting to see the results, he limped over to grab the war club from the other side of the room.

The dwarf leaned against the desk, clutching at the yew shaft that jutted from its chest. Where the dwarf's hands touched it, his hand smoked and smoldered, as did the flesh around where the wound. The Avartagh looked fearfully at Colin as he advanced across the room.

Colin smiled in grim satisfaction as he limped slowly toward the Avartagh, dragging the club with one hand behind him while he enjoyed the creature's terror. With every limping step, the bat made a metallic sound as it scraped on the tile floor of the office. Step-drag-*skritch*. Step-drag-*skritch*. Step-drag-*skritch*.

The Avartagh's eyes widened in fear with each step Colin took toward him, and he began to bargain for his life.

"I really do have gold, boy—riches beyond measure. I can make sure your mother and you never have to worry about money, ever again. I can even make her a famous artist. Just spare me from going back to the grave. I can't go back—I won't!"

Colin ignored the Avartagh's cries for mercy. Finally, he was within reach, and firmly grasped the handle of his lucky bat with both hands.

"Let's get something straight, you disgusting little freak of a creature. You hurt my mom. You hurt my friend! *You hurt my town.* And I think it's time to put you back in the dirt, once and for all."

He raised the bat high overhead like a samurai, and the dwarf cringed as Colin crunched it down on his head. When the bat struck, an earth-shattering sound emitted from the meeting of bat and dwarf noggin. Colin staggered back several feet from to the impact and barely managed to stay upright. After catching his balance, he looked up to see that the Avartagh's body was shriveling and shrinking. The vampire seemed to deflate right in front of his eyes, aging hundreds upon hundreds of years in a matter of seconds. Soon, all that was left was a withered, mummified corpse.

Remembering the mayor, Colin limped as fast as he could behind the desk to check on him. He was bleeding profusely from where he'd pulled the crossbow bolt from his shoulder, so Colin removed his hoodie and used it to apply direct pressure to the mayor's wound. "I'm sorry I had to do that, Mayor Boynton. Please don't die."

He pulled out his phone and dialed 9-1-1 to call for an ambulance, then promptly passed into unconsciousness.

When he woke Colin was in a hospital room, surrounded by flowers and cards. He had tubes sticking out of both arms, a plastic tube hanging out of his side, an oxygen mask on his face, and several I.V. bags were hanging from metal poles next to the bed. As he fully opened his eyes and looked around, he saw Jesse sleeping in a chair in the corner, and his mom asleep in a chair right next to her.

He tried to sit up but found it was incredibly painful to move. Recalling when he'd had his tonsils removed as a child, he found the controls for the bed and adjusted it so he was sitting upright. As he did, both his mom and Jesse woke up, and his mother cried as she rushed to his side.

"You're awake! Oh, thank God—the doctors said it was best to keep you under, but I thought you'd never wake up again!"

He squeezed his mother's hand and smiled at her. "I'm fine, Mom—or at least I think I'll heal up alright. Just give me a few days." She leaned down and kissed him on the forehead.

"A few days?" Jesse waved at him from behind Mrs. McCool's shoulder and winked. "When you *saved* the *mayor* from the *tornado*, you suffered two broken ribs, a collapsed lung, a sprained ankle, a broken hand, and a concussion—not to mention thirty-four stitches and the most wicked collection of scrapes and bruises I have ever seen."

Since Jesse was standing behind his mom, she'd emphasized the details of the cover story with finger quotes. Colin got the picture and decided to play it dumb by faking a case of amnesia. "Huh. I don't remember any of that. How long was I out?"

"It's Monday, so you've been out for about two days now. The doctors were actually keeping you under for the first day so you could rest. But they stopped drugging you last night, and your mom and I worried you'd never wake up." Jesse reached past his mom and punched him ever so lightly on the arm. "Anyway, you're the town hero now. Check out all the cards and flowers. Looks like you're going to be the big man on campus, for a while at least."

"Jesse, keep an eye on him while I let the staff know he's awake," Colin's mom stated. Then she scurried off out of the room, calling for the nurse as she scampered down the hall.

Colin winced as he readjusted in bed, and turned to look at Jesse. "So, I'm glad to see that you're alright. I passed out, and the last thing I thought of was going to find you."

Jesse shrugged her shoulders. "Eh, no need. I got jumped by that miniature nightmare right when you went into the mayor's office, and that's when the little freak made the switch. I woke up in a storage closet, but cut myself loose before the cheerleaders from hell arrived. Then, I kicked their prissy little powder puff butts all over the place. Turns out an iron crow bar can give the fair folk a bad case of the see ya laters. Who knew? Anyway, by the time I got back upstairs you and the mayor were surrounded by paramedics. They say you saved his life."

"Well, I'm glad he's okay, since I was nearly responsible for killing him." He moved slightly and winced. "I guess that dwarf was pretty tough after all."

Jesse smiled and punched him again on the shoulder, which elicited a grimace from Colin. "When you get better, I wanna hear how you took out the vampire dwarf—and nearly killed the mayor in the process."

"Hey, you're the one who shot the mayor." Colin chuckled and then winced as he leaned his head back on the pillow. "Honestly, though, right now all I want to do is sleep. Wake me when it's time for dinner," he mumbled as he closed his eyes, and soon drifted off with a peaceful look on his battered face.

Jesse leaned in and planted a gentle peck on his cheek. "You do that, slugger. I think you earned it."

19

Colin spent two weeks in the hospital recuperating. At first, the doctors wanted to keep him longer due to the extent of his injuries. But, Finnegas snuck him an herbal concoction that sped up the healing process considerably, leading his doctors to declare his recovery a medical mystery. They also asked him to return for further studies, an offer which his mother first respectfully, then forcefully, declined.

As he got better, Jesse and Finnegas filled him in on what had happened in the days since his confrontation with the evil dwarf. Immediately after Colin had killed the Avartagh, Finnegas had gotten help from a real leprechaun in casting another spell on the town. This time it was to convince them that a tornado had swept through, which provided an explanation for all the damage and disarray. As Finnegas said, it was a thin excuse, but people seemed to believe what they wanted to believe, regardless of any evidence to the contrary.

Moreover, he'd enlisted the help of the local brownie clan to clean the accumulated filth from everyone's homes, which served to cover up for the weeks the townsfolk had spent neglecting them. Finnegas and a few of the more amenable fae had also spent a few days tying up loose ends and plugging the holes in their cover story. Since then, everyone in the town had pretty much returned to their old lives. Thankfully, no one had a clue that they'd lived in a fantasy world for the better part of the last several weeks.

By the time Colin got out of the hospital, the town was looking much more like the one he remembered. Also his ankle was healed up enough to get around, and his ribs and hand were on the mend as well, thanks to the nasty-tasting but potent healing potion Finnegas had been making him drink every day. After a day spent at home doing nothing he complained of boredom, so Jesse offered to take him to see her dad's new place of work.

Before he'd lost his job, Mr. Callahan had done something that had to do with accounting and bookkeeping, but that's all Colin knew.

Colin was relieved to know that Jesse's dad had found a new job, but he didn't understand what that had to do with him.

"Jesse, I'm really glad your dad is working and all, but I don't understand why you want me to go see where he works. I'm tired of being indoors—can't we just go hang out at the park?"

She arched an eyebrow at him, as if to say he wasn't getting out of it no matter how much he complained. "I know you've been cooped up for weeks, and you don't want to visit some boring old office. But trust me when I say you're going to want to see this."

Since neither teen owned a car, Colin's mom dropped them off downtown. They walked the short distance to the warehouse district where most of the shipping and manufacturing businesses were located. Soon the pair turned a corner and walked up to a tidy-looking warehouse with a brown brick façade. Over the door was a small green sign with gold lettering that said "Éire Imports."

Colin at his friend. "You have got to be kidding me."

Jesse smiled and opened the door with a flourish of her hand as she bowed with mock courtesy. "After you."

They walked into a small reception area, where a young and attractive red-headed receptionist sat behind the counter. She seemed to know Jesse fairly well and greeted them with a smile, pointing with her thumb to an entrance behind her.

"Your dad's in his office, Jesse," she said. Then she seemed to notice Colin for the first time, at which point she looked him over appraisingly. "And this must be the handsome hero who saved the mayor. Glad to see you're up and about."

Jesse smiled, eager at the opportunity to make introductions. "Colin, this is Maureen, the receptionist here at Éire Imports." She nudged him gently and spoke quietly to him out of the side of her mouth. "Um, manners? Say something, nerd."

Despite himself, Colin blushed. The receptionist was pretty and spoke with an Irish brogue, which Colin thought made her extra hot, and he just wasn't used to receiving attention from attractive girls. Well, except for Jesse, but he'd never tell her that he thought she was attractive. He coughed into his hand nervously and smiled.

"Um, thank you, miss. I'm just glad the mayor is okay. I mean, after the—tragedy."

The receptionist grinned pleasantly, then went back to her work as she replied. "Well, I'm sure it's nothing that time and a little spell of forgetting won't fix."

Colin gave Jesse a questioning look, but Jesse just smirked and shook her head. "C'mon, let's go say hi to my dad and his new *boss*."

Jesse shoved Colin through the doorway and down a hall until they got to an office where Jesse's dad sat behind a desk, tapping away furiously at a computer keyboard.

"Hi, Dad!" Jesse blurted with giddiness as they strolled into the office. It was apparent how glad she was that her dad was still gainfully employed. He remembered what it had been like for his family when his dad had died, and knew how stressful it could be when you weren't sure where the next month's house payment or groceries were coming from.

Mr. Callahan looked up and smiled. "Jesse—and Colin! What a surprise, come in, come in. Do you two want a soda or some water?" He turned and gestured toward a mini-fridge behind him. Colin looked around and took in his office. To be honest, it was pretty posh; it looked like Jesse's dad had landed a pretty decent gig.

Jesse waved off her dad's offer, which irritated Colin, since he was actually kind of thirsty. "Is Mr. Murphy around?"

Her dad nodded. "He is—and in fact he said to stop by to see him. Something about a book you wanted to borrow for a school assignment?"

"Yep. Thanks, Dad—I'll go talk to him and introduce Colin. We'll swing by before we leave."

"Okay, let me know if you need a ride home."

"Thanks, Dad!" Jesse saluted him, then dragged Colin farther down the hall. "Wait till you meet Dad's new boss—you're going to flip."

"Why do I have a funny feeling I know him already?" he replied.

20

As they walked further down the hall, Colin recognized a familiar scent—a combination of pipe smoke, peat moss, and black tea. When they walked into the large office at the end of the hall Finnegas was there, puffing away on his pipe. He sat behind an enormous oak desk, polished to a sheen and detailed with elaborate scrollwork and carvings of dragons, horses, and various other wild beasts and creatures.

"Ah, there you are—and none the worse for the wear, I see. Looks as though the healing draught I gave you did the trick." He winked, and frankly Colin thought it made him look like a skinny Santa Claus. He wondered for a moment if Santa Claus was real, too.

"Now, about that book you wanted to borrow." He turned to the wall behind him, which was covered floor to ceiling in books, many of which appeared to be quite old. "Ah yes, *Celtic Myths and Legends*—here it is. This should serve nicely as a primer for what you two can expect to be facing in the future." He handed the book over to Jesse from across the desk.

Colin perked up at that remark and put his hands up in protest. "Wait a minute—just how far in the future do you mean by 'in the future'? I figured since we took care of the Avartagh, that would be it for a while. You did notice that I almost died recently?"

Finnegas waved his protests off and gestured sternly at the chairs in front of his desk. "Sit, sit, the both of you. There'll be enough time to talk about that later."

Colin decided not to press the issue and sat down, swiveling his eyes around to check out the druid's office. Shields and swords decorated the walls, as well as tapestries depicting battles from what he assumed were stories out of legend. He nodded appreciatively.

"So, this is your cover identity—pretty slick."

The old man waved him off with an annoyed look. "Bah, you read too many comics. This is my livelihood. I've run this business since before you were born, right here from this office and building. Being a druid may have its perks, but it doesn't pay very well, I'll tell you that."

Colin managed to look properly chastised and nodded. "So, you live here in town?"

Finnegas took a puff from his pipe and pointed at Colin with it. "Quite right. As I said, I've looked after the McCool family for quite some time. When your mother and father settled here many years ago, I moved my import-export business here so I could keep an eye on them. Your father actually worked for me for a few years after he left the service the first time, back before he re-upped when the war broke out."

Colin wasn't exactly stunned, but this was all news to him. He merely nodded and sat pensively as the old man spoke. Meanwhile, Jesse looked like a kid on Christmas morning, barely reining in her excitement as she bounced up and down on the edge of her seat.

"Can I show him the back now, Finnegas? Please?"

He frowned slightly and rolled his eyes in mock annoyance. "Oh, I suppose." Then his expression grew much more serious. "But don't touch anything. Neither of you have started your training yet, and much of what I have back there is quite dangerous. So, no horsing around."

Jesse nodded. "I'll keep bat boy here in check, scout's honor." She held up her right hand in a mock scout salute, and tugged on Colin's arm as she jumped out of her seat and headed to the door.

Colin protested weakly as she pulled him along. "But wait—I have questions! And what does he mean by 'starting our training'?"

Finnegas shooed them away. "As I said, there'll be plenty of time for that later. I'll come find you once the lass has shown you the sights."

Jesse led him through a door and into a hall that was just beyond the old druid's office. They walked through a large warehouse area that was filled floor to ceiling with crates and boxes, many of which had markings indicating they'd been shipped from overseas. Other than that, the place looked pretty typical. It was just your basic warehouse with a forklift, boxes of stuff, and not much else.

"Okay, this looks pretty boring. I don't get what the big deal is."

Jesse winked at him. "Uh-huh. Well check *this* out, smarty pants." She walked down a corridor made by two rows of floor-to-ceiling crates and stopped at the end. There, a tall wooden crate sat flush against the wall. She depressed a brick in the wall next to it, and the front of the crate swung out like a door.

Colin nodded. "Okay, a secret door. I'll admit that's pretty slick. But what's behind it?"

Jesse turned to him with a grin. "Oh, you haven't seen anything yet." She ducked into the crate and Colin followed. To box opened into a short passageway though the wall, which led to a concrete hallway roughly ten feet long and six feet wide. Fluorescent lights illuminated the space, and an arched doorway and an iron-plated door of imposing proportions sat at its end. The door was locked with an enormous padlock, and a key hung right next to the door on a hook.

"That's some security system old Finnegas has here. All that trouble to hide this place, and the key is sitting out in plain sight. Brilliant."

Jesse thumped him on the skull with her middle finger. "Duh! No one can see the key but us, just like only people like us can see the fair folk. Also, Finnegas says the iron door keeps them out. Apparently, the fae *really* hate cold iron."

That had Colin sucking on his thumb, thinking back to when he'd first seen the war club's true shape. Now it looked just like his old bat again, but he clearly remembered the large iron rings that banded the ends of the club, and the metallic scraping sound it had made when he dragged it across the floor of the mayor's office.

Jesse turned the key in the lock and removed it, and struggled to open the door. "A little help here? The hinges need oiling—Finnegas says no one has been back here since—well, since before your dad died."

Colin tried not to react to that information, and quietly helped her open the door. Behind it was a large room, about forty feet square, obviously part of the building next door to the warehouse. Jesse flipped a switch on the wall and the light fixtures slowly lit up overhead, just like in the gymnasium at school. The floors were polished wood—oak, from the look of them. There were skylights above in the high ceiling, letting in plenty of natural light, and somehow he felt like he belonged there.

As he looked around, it was plain to see what the space was for; this was a place to train warriors. Colin had no doubt about it. There were wooden swords and other practice weapons in racks along one wall, and shields too. On the far side of the room, an archery range was set up, along with a larger target for practicing spear throwing. Along another wall were several posts wrapped in thick bands of rope on wooden bases. Colin recognized these from a report he'd written on medieval combat as 'pells,' which were used for practicing striking in sword fighting.

In addition to the weapons areas, there was also a space with mats, similar to the martial arts flooring his dad had used to have in their garage at home. Here there were punching bags, kicking shields, and mitts for striking, as well as more esoteric martial arts weapons of the type he'd seen used in Asian martial arts movies.

There was a plaque on the far wall above the equipment, with writing in an old-looking language that at first he couldn't understand. Above the writing there was a strange triangular symbol over a sword crossed with a staff. After he looked at the sign for a moment or two he somehow knew what it meant, although he couldn't quite say how. Translated, the plaque read:

Truth in our hearts.

Strength in our hands.

Actions to match our words.

It sounded exactly like something his dad had used to tell him. Colin's eyes began to well with tears.

21

He wiped his eyes and turned to face his friend. "My dad used to train here, didn't he?"

Jesse shyly looked away, as if reluctant to answer his question. "I think so. Finnegas said he'd explain it all to you when you got released from the hospital." She paused and gave Colin a serious look. "From the looks of it, your dad was more than a soldier, Colin. I'm pretty sure he was one of the fianna, just like Finnegas said."

They heard a voice from behind them. "Indeed, he was a *rígfénnid*, a leader of a fian." Somehow, Finnegas had snuck in behind them without their noticing. "And, he was a good man."

Colin could see the obvious sadness on the old man's face. "So I guess you knew my dad pretty well." He said it as a statement more than a question.

Finnegas nodded once. "Aye, I trained him, from the time he was about your age I suppose. He was fierce, but kind, and given over more to mercy than I might have liked. It cost him dearly in the end." He looked at Colin as if to make a point.

Colin met the old man's gaze with a confidence he'd not known before the events of the previous week. "But, why? I mean, what did you train him for?"

The old druid looked impatient, which Colin was beginning to realize was his default setting when questioned by curious teenagers. "Why do you think? Do you think this is the first time that the fair folk have meddled in human affairs? Do you think they're content to be pushed aside by humanity, who once worshipped them as gods? No, they were always fickle and filled with spite, especially those more powerful than your garden variety brownie or hobgoblin. It's those more dangerous and malicious representatives of the fair folk that the fianna have always protected humankind against. That's why."

Colin was sucking his thumb furiously, which didn't seem to bother Finnegas at all. Jesse piped in with a question that had been bothering Colin as well. "I don't understand, Finnegas—why do they hate us so much?"

The druid sat down on a wooden bench and began packing his pipe with tobacco. He looked up and gestured with his pipe as he responded. "It's not necessarily hate that drives them, although some clearly do hate mankind. But for the most part, it's just in their nature to do us harm." He paused to light his pipe, and continued. "Ever been to the zoo?"

"Sure, lots of times."

"Seen the gorillas? Maybe a tiger or a lion?"

Jesse and Colin looked at each other. "Of course," Colin replied.

"And, people take care of them, right? But do their caretakers treat them like people?" He sat back and puffed on his pipe, content to wait on a response.

"Well, no. I mean, they're not people—they're dangerous animals."

The old man nodded. "Would you say, unpredictable, even?" Both of them nodded likewise in response, and the old man continued. "Yet people are still fascinated with wild creatures, and those who are unfamiliar with them want to ascribe to them human traits. But they are *not* human. Certainly, wild animals can become fond of humans, and in rare instances bond with them on a certain level. But never should a person make the mistake that they are anything but wild. That is the closest thing in our world that I can compare with the nature of the *aés sidhe*. Wild. Unpredictable. And, dangerous."

He breathed out billowy clouds of fragrant smoke, and went on. "What makes the fair folk most dangerous, though, is the fact that they often look so much like you and me. That in turn makes us want to think of them as being like us—we tend to think they have human traits and emotions. But, I can tell you for a certainty, they do *not* share our emotions. In fact, they are as alien in mind and heart to you and me as a shark is to a puppy. You should also know that many are highly intelligent, and even those that aren't have had millennia to become cunning and devious enough to make up for it. Not a one of them can be trusted."

The old man blew out puffs of smoke through his nose, which

made Colin reflect that without magical assistance, he'd have died of lung cancer long ago. "But that still doesn't answer my question. Why do they want to hurt us?"

"Why not? They see themselves as superior to us. To them, we are like ants, or at best little toys to be played with and tossed aside at their whim and fancy. And, after centuries or even millennia of living, they simply grow bored. If you've ever seen a mean-spirited child pull a leg off a grasshopper, just to see it hop around in a circle, then you have some idea of why they do what they do."

Jesse and Colin sat down on the bench beside Finnegas. Colin didn't look at the old man as he spoke, but instead stared out into the training hall. "So I suppose you want me to fight them, like my dad did."

Finnegas shook his head remorsefully. "My boy, if I could spare you from it, I would. However, you're marked by druid blood, and the fair folk are drawn to your family like iron filings to a magnet. You could travel to the ends of the earth, and they'd still follow you and meddle in your affairs, playing their cruel tricks simply to watch you jump around in circles. Whether you choose to accept it or not, it is your destiny, although I hesitate to use such a grand term to describe what amounts to a rough lot in life.

"I'll not sugar-coat it for you, boy: *McCool men die young.* I've rarely seen a McCool live to see the far side of fifty, although not for a lack of preparation, that's for sure. I'll do everything I can to prepare you for what lies ahead, but your life is bound to be filled with battles against the fae, from now until they lay you to rest. And that's the raw truth of it."

Colin gave the old man a quizzical look. "So what's the upside to all this? I mean, there has to be something of benefit here."

"Spoken with the true attitude of youth, who assume they'll live forever no matter what." He nodded and grinned. "Well, the training is tough, and as I said the pay for druids is not great. But you'll develop skills that most people could only dream of."

"Meaning…"

"Meaning, you'll learn to use magic. Not to master it, mind you, but you'll learn the most basic of spells, the ones most likely to be of use. And, you'll learn how to fight, whether empty-handed or with weapons. Finally, as you mature you'll find you're a bit stronger and faster than the average person, and more resilient as well."

Colin frowned. "You told me I didn't have super powers."

Finnegas rolled his eyes. "You don't, at least not like some fae. No, you're just a bit hardier than the average human. Some say it's genetics, while others say human champions are blessed by powers beyond mortal comprehension. Regardless, as you grow into manhood you'll become that much harder to kill."

Colin looked peeved. "Man, you mean I have to fight evil elves and save the world, and I don't even get super powers? This blows."

Jesse snickered behind her hands, while Finnegas merely looked at him in mock disapproval. "I dare say you're not ready to save the world yet, boy. You've a lot of training ahead of you."

Colin looked genuinely offended. "But I just did!"

"That was a fluke, and if I'd had my way you'd never have been put in that situation without adequate training. However, the Avartagh's escape was unplanned and unexpected, and I honestly thought it would take him another decade to chase down all the rabbit trails and false leads I'd set up for him."

Colin narrowed his eyes. "So that's what you were doing after Dad died."

"Yes, but a fat lot of good it did." He stopped and raised a finger in exclamation. "Oh! There's one thing I forgot to mention—you do get to choose some help." He then looked over at Jesse expectantly.

Jesse jumped up and pointed a finger in Colin's face. "Guess what, bat boy? You're stuck with me." She grinned from ear to ear, and placed her hands on her hips as if to dare him to argue about it.

Colin shook his head. "I don't know if I want to put someone else in harm's way like this. I mean, it's bad enough that I have to do this stuff. How could I live with myself if something happened to anyone else?"

Finnegas shrugged. "Well, it's too late for that. Once you chose to involve her in your quest, her fate became inextricably entwined with your own, and she's as much a part of your fianna now as you are." He smiled and patted Colin on the shoulder. "Congratulations, you're the first rígfénnid in generations to choose a female warrior as your lieutenant."

Jesse turned to Colin with her hand held high and with a huge grin plastered across her face. "High five for women's lib!"

Colin ignored her enthusiasm and rubbed his face in his hands. "Man, what have I gotten myself into?"

22

The next day, Finnegas picked them up after church in an old pickup truck, and took them out to a remote section of hills in the woods beyond the park.

Colin knew wherever they were going, it must have had something to do with the events of the previous weeks. "So, are you going to tell us what's up?"

"I thought you'd want to be around to see the Avartagh laid to rest for the final time," he replied. "This is actually part of your training—you need to see how it's done, in case this ever happens again. Which, after today, I doubt will be a problem. But it never hurts to be prepared."

"Speaking of which—where are we going to find the time to do all this training you have planned?"

The druid harrumphed as he pulled down what looked to be a freshly-made dirt road. "Didn't the lass tell you? You're both working for me now, as warehouse help. That should be a sufficient cover story for you, especially with Jesse's dad working in my employ as well."

Colin snickered. "You're a sneaky old coot, you know that?"

The old man nodded. "The sneakiest. It comes with the territory." They pulled into a clearing on top of a low hill, where a large hole had been recently excavated with large machinery. "Now, help me unload the crate before the concrete truck gets here."

They got out and walked to the back of the old pickup, where Finnegas pulled back a large tarp to expose a metal box roughly the size of small refrigerator. The box was wrapped in chains, and those were secured with heavy locks the size of Colin's meaty fists. Someone had written 'this side down' on the outside of the box, with an arrow pointing in the direction the box should be buried.

"I took the liberty of preparing this while you were holed up in the hospital. He's been wrapped in iron chains, bound in iron shackles, and once he's in the ground we'll plant briars so thick around this area no one will ever know it's here." They attached the box upside down to a hook on the end of an excavator that sat off to the side of the hole in the ground. Finnegas worked the controls from the cab, and lowered the box into the ground. Jesse had to climb on the shovel to release the box, but otherwise it went off without a hitch.

Colin looked down into the pit, which was quite deep. He estimated that the Avartagh would be surrounded by at least five feet of concrete on all sides, even on the bottom, since someone had cleverly lined the bottom and sides of the pit with concrete rebar, so the box was nestled firmly off the bottom by about two feet. He'd be encased in a cold grave of iron and concrete, which Colin guessed would hold him long after he was dead, which was fine by him.

They stood around and watched as a concrete truck pulled in and backed up to the hole to deliver its contents. The workers never said a word, and never even bothered to look in the pit to see what they were covering. Or, if they did, they never said anything about it.

Jesse arched an eyebrow at the strange behavior of the workmen. The old man spoke softly as he explained. "These gentlemen work for a rather industrious criminal enterprise in the city. Their boss owes me several favors, and a generous payday combined with some simple illusory magic means they'll never tell a soul what happened here today."

Colin shook his head. "I don't even want to know how you got mixed up with the mob. In fact, I'm going to pretend I didn't hear that last part."

When the job was finished and the concrete crew had left, Colin breathed a huge sigh of relief. "Well, I'm glad that's over with."

The old man laughed as he lit his pipe. "Enjoy this brief respite while you can—I'm sure we'll be dealing with some other mess brought on by the fair folk and their mischief in no time." He waggled his eyebrows comically at them. "Now, who's in the mood for burgers and shakes? All this skullduggery always makes me work up an appetite." He headed over to the truck without waiting for an answer.

Jesse went to follow, but Colin stopped her with a gentle hand on her arm. "You sure you're ready for all this? I mean, I bet if you wanted to back out we could figure something out."

She punched him lightly on the arm and smiled a slightly wicked grin. "What, and let you have all the fun? This is the most excitement we've had in this town in, like, forever! No way I'm missing out. Like I said, slugger—you're stuck with me."

Colin tried to hold back a grin and failed. "Fair enough. I call shotgun!"

"Not if I get there first!" She grabbed his arm and twisted while sweeping his feet out from under him, leaving him in a pile in the dirt.

"No fair! I'm still gimped up. And no beating up the local hero!" Jesse's laughter trailed off as she bolted toward the truck.

Colin stood up and dusted off his jeans. "Well, it was fun having her sympathy while it lasted," he muttered, under his breath. He spared a final glance at the grave of the Avartagh, then followed after her, smiling and thinking that he could do worse for a best friend than Jesse Callahan.

Epilogue

Nearly 4,000 miles away, an enormous dragon sat and brooded silently in a cave beneath a deep Irish lake. She was old, older than most of the creatures that inhabited the lands, and far older than any human, druid or otherwise. The old *wyrm* shifted her weight, and as she did, huge chains rattled against the floor of the cavern. The chains were attached to her body with great collars and cuffs at her neck and ankles, and again at the other end into massive eyelets that were sunk deep into the stone walls.

The *dullahan* walked through the huge iron doors that blocked the entrance to the cave, for there were few doors on earth that could block his passage. He strode unafraid to within striking distance of her tail and claws, and certainly within lethal distance of her fiery breath, then knelt before her. When he spoke, his voice didn't come from the decapitated head he carried under his arm. Instead, it seemed to emanate from the large gaping hole in his shoulders where his neck should have been, and it sounded like broken glass crunching under a horse's hooves. "The dwarf has fallen."

She turned her huge head to fix her yellow slitted eyes on him, and as she did puffs of smoke blew from her nostrils. Her lips never moved, but the *dullahan* heard her voice speak to him just the same. Despite his evil nature, it chilled his bones to hear it.

Did he find the book?

"No. He failed to locate it. The *cat sith* say the boy does not have it."

Then the old man has it. Go. Retrieve it. We must have it to break the seals.

"It will be done." He bowed his head again, then stood and departed from the cavern. The *dullahan* vowed he would not fail his mother. Soon, she'd be free to roam the earth again, and his kind would rule as gods once more.

***

Want more Colin McCool?

Go to MDMassey.com to get the next book in the Colin McCool paranormal suspense series, Junkyard Druid! And while you're there, be sure to sign up for my newsletter to download another *free* book!